# Wade  shower stall.

His wet, black hair was slicked back. Water beads dotted his tanned broad shoulders in a chaotic and intoxicating manner. Even though he stood sideways, Jessie could see the moisture glistening in the dark hair that covered his chest. Tiny rivulets ran down his body, over the flat planes of his stomach, the narrow curve of his back and the taut muscles of his buttocks. She couldn't move, couldn't think. She could only stare at Wade Brooks...at all of Wade Brooks.

"What the hell?"

Jessie's eyes collided with his steely blue ones. Sparks skittered along her spine. *Look him in the eye!* Too aware of his sleek, sinewy, totally naked body, she glued her gaze to his. But every rational thought went right down the drain. "Wh-what a surprise to find you here!"

He scowled, a look that sent intense awareness through her veins.

Perspiration broke out along her upper lip. *Oh, God, he's not covering himself with a towel. Now what do I do?* "I d-didn't mean to intrude on your shower. But I've tried more c-conventional ways of getting in touch with you. You're a hard man—" Her eyes dipped to his very male, very naked...

Wade raised a cynical brow.

"I mean you're a *difficult* man to get a hold of."

Dear Reader,

Having written traditional romances for the last few years, I was surprised when Jessie Hart, the heroine of *Bachelor Blues*, turned out to be anything but traditional. From the beginning, she was self-confident, sassy and a little too daring for her own good. She even followed the hero into the men's locker room and interrupted his shower! I knew then she was trouble—and the kind of woman Temptation readers could identify with.

I guess I must have a wild streak in me, too—I couldn't resist writing this book. I've been a Temptation reader for many years and am thrilled to be writing for this wonderful line. I hope you have as much fun reading *Bachelor Blues* as I had writing it!

Enjoy,

*LeAnna Wilson*

## Books by Leanna Wilson

**SILHOUETTE ROMANCE**

Don't miss any of our special offers. Write to us at the following address for information on our newest releases.

Harlequin Reader Service
U.S.: 3010 Walden Ave., P.O. Box 1325, Buffalo, NY 14269
Canadian: P.O. Box 609, Fort Erie, Ont. L2A 5X3

# BACHELOR BLUES
## Leanna Wilson

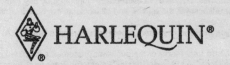

HARLEQUIN®

TORONTO • NEW YORK • LONDON
AMSTERDAM • PARIS • SYDNEY • HAMBURG
STOCKHOLM • ATHENS • TOKYO • MILAN • MADRID
PRAGUE • WARSAW • BUDAPEST • AUCKLAND

For Graham,
You are a true blessing!
I love you more than you will ever know.

Acknowledgments

Thanks Dorothy! I love brainstorming with you!!!
Judy Christenberry, thank you for your generosity of spirit.

ISBN 0-373-25863-1

BACHELOR BLUES

Copyright © 2000 by Leanna Ellis.

# 1

"SOUL MATES?" Jessie Hart gave a disbelieving shake of her head. "Isn't that too lofty a promise to our customers?"

Jack, her twin brother, propped his bare feet on the new receptionist's desk that had been delivered earlier that day. The frayed ends of his jeans snaked over his lean brown ankles. He gave a sly grin. It was the kind that had attracted women from all walks of life. It amused Jessie to watch women chase after him as desperately as they chased down bargains at Macy's. It was something she'd never do.

"If we're going to do this," Jack said, "then let's do it right. I don't want a run-of-the-mill dating service."

"How can we offer to find someone's soul mate?" The thought of soul mates and a life-long commitment made her insides shift uncomfortably. "I don't want to be a pessimist, but what if someone's soul mate isn't one of our customers? I think that's a pretty tall order to fill."

"Give me some credit." He propped his hands behind his head. "I hooked up Rachel and Greg, didn't I?"

Rachel Simmons had dated Jack when they were in college. Instead of dumping her when she pressed for a commitment, he found someone more to her liking, someone ready to say "I do." Unimpressed with that feat, Jessie shrugged. "That was a fluke."

"How about Amanda and Steve?" he returned.

"Lucky guess. You didn't want Amanda anymore and wanted out of that relationship. Steve happened to be one of your fraternity brothers, single, good-looking, and willing to commit."

"And he also happened to be her soul mate. They said so at their wedding, remember?" He dusted the tips of his fingers against an imaginary lapel as if he'd performed a flawless magic trick. "I believe they gave one of us credit for their falling in love and getting married." Jack's green eyes glimmered mischievously. "And it wasn't you."

Not about to concede a point, she countered, "Look at Tony and Gwen. They're separated now. Guess they weren't soul mates." Concern made her frown. "If they'd been our clients, could they hold us liable?"

"No. Besides, they reconciled. They flew to Fiji last week to renew their vows."

So much for that argument.

Why did she feel her stomach twist each time she heard another happy ending—especially one that her brother had instigated? It wasn't that she wished anyone ill. Besides, it had been her idea to capitalize on Jack's innate and well-renowned ability to match-make.

Happy endings were good, right? In the dating business she and her brother were starting, cases of happily-ever-after certainly gave them more credibility. Jack had an impeccable record with those he'd matched together, which meant more clients and more profits.

The skin between her brows pinched tight. Maybe

her skepticism was because she didn't understand the insatiable need to find a mate, to pair up and off, to say "I do." Storybook endings just weren't for her. When she was a little girl, her mother read her the classic fairy tales, but instead of Cinderella, Snow White or Sleeping Beauty marrying the handsome prince, they went off on their own to establish careers as doctors, lawyers or financiers.

"Passionate relationships are often stormy," Jack added, interrupting her thoughts.

"Thank you, Oprah, for that insight." She knew all about tempestuous relationships, having seen her parents spar with each other over the years. Even though they'd divorced when she and Jack were babies, they'd squared off at family events or when they'd swap twins for summer vacation.

The divorce settlement had separated Jack and Jessie, putting more than a thousand miles between them. Nina Hart had taken her daughter away from L.A. to Dallas and taught her self-respect, self-reliance and self-confidence. Jack had stayed with their father and his string of new brides, the latest being two years younger than Jessie.

She'd relished the quiet of her mother's chic condo compared to her father's overbuilt, overcrowded house where she had more half brothers and sisters than she could count. Yet she'd always felt as if a part of her were missing. She'd found that piece at Stanford where she and Jack had reunited.

Immediately, they'd become best friends. It was as if two halves had been put back together. She'd gained a new, sometimes baffling, perspective. She'd helped him focus on his studies when he'd have rather been partying, and he'd helped her spread her wings, live a little, experience life. She hadn't realized she'd missed so much while holed up in the library or in front of her computer terminal. In four short years, they'd made up for the eighteen they'd been separated.

They'd often talked of teaming up in business, but the idea sparking their dating service had taken five more years after graduation to catch fire. They'd both done equally well in their prospective careers by then and were financially at a point where they could break away from corporate life and start their own business together.

"Don't look so disappointed that Tony and Gwen are back together," Jack said, narrowing his eyes on her in the annoying way he did when he was reading her thoughts.

"I'm not." In fact, she'd initially thought Gwen could have used the separation as an opportunity to concentrate on her career, without Tony complaining about how much time she spent working overtime. "I just thought—"

"Love isn't predictable, Jess."

Why not? she wondered. "How hard could it be to figure out if two people are compatible?"

"I'm not talking about getting along. I'm talking about passion. Unmistakable, uncontrollable passion. Where your heart beats wildly when you're near or just thinking about that special someone. When you can't think about anything else. Can't eat or sleep or function without the other."

"You make it sound like a disease."

He frowned. "Didn't you ever feel that with...what was the name of that last guy you went out with for so long?"

"Parker." And no, he hadn't consumed her

thoughts or time. Even though they'd practically lived together for more than a year, they'd maintained their separate and distinct lives, no strings, no demands. Nice, civil, easy. "We were perfect together."

"Is that why he dumped you?"

Sometimes Jack was exasperating. "Did not."

"Did, too."

She shrugged, not feeling any resentment or sadness about Parker. "That's why it was the perfect relationship. When we parted—mutually—we were each able to go on with our lives without being devastated."

"Uh-huh. Sounds so romantic. So boring." Jack gave her one of his charming grins. "I can't wait to watch you fall head over heels for some guy."

The corners of her mouth pinching into a frown, she nudged his bare foot with her elbow. "Let's get back to work. We need to settle on a promo."

"We could have a huge gala for our Grand Opening. Sort of a fraternity party where singles could meet each other."

"I'm not sold on that. But we still have time to decide."

He rubbed his unshaven jaw. "We need something catchy for the company name. Something to set us apart from all the other dating services in Dallas."

The sunlight shining through the front window made her brother's hair shimmer like gold. In more ways than hair color and gender, Jessie had always recognized their stark differences. He was laid-back. She was a workaholic. He liked pizza and beer. She preferred linguini and white wine. He loved the outdoors. She opted for air-conditioning and her computer terminal. But their opposing interests matched up well for business. Their personalities complimented each other, each having their own gifts and assets.

Jack dragged his fingers through his hair. "We're the *Hello Dolly* of the new millennium. Our approach is more personal, with me making the matches, you, the introductions. No computers."

"No what?" she bristled.

"No computers," he repeated. "No videos. No thumbing through photos. But we need something more. Something to really set us apart. To show we're not just another dating service where lonely and desperate people go as a last resort. We want people to think of us first when it comes to love and romance."

She shifted in her seat, uncomfortable with his thoughts. She wanted something reliable, tangible, concrete. What was wrong with computer matches? They didn't have to hook people up randomly, as in "The next on the list goes with number three-twelve." She bit her lip. "You don't like 'Heart to Heart'?"

He gave a comical grimace. "Reminds me of that TV show."

"Isn't name recognition a great advertising tool?"

Suddenly he jerked his feet to the floor and leaned forward. "Think about this. Soul Mates." He snapped his fingers and pointed to the bottom of his foot. "Sole mates. Get it? S-o-l-e. It's different. It's hip. I can see the logo. 'Want someone to put their shoes under your bed...permanently?'" He waggled his eyebrows. "Sexy, eh?"

Jess wrinkled her nose. "Not a pretty picture."

"I'm talking kismet, fate, that there is no one else in this world that completes you like the person we're going to set you up with. A matching set. A perfect pair."

Doubtful, she arched a brow. "Of espadrilles? Clogs? Stilettos?"

"It works. Goes great with my theory about love and shoes." He paused, waiting for her reaction.

She took a gulp of cold coffee. "Go ahead. You're going to tell me anyway, even if I don't want to hear it."

"You're cynical."

She grinned. "Optimism is highly overrated." Containing her smile, she gave a serious nod. "What's your theory?"

He gave an aloof shrug, hiding his enthusiasm, but she could see the fire in his green eyes, his passion for the topic. "It's how I've matched every couple. Amanda and Steve—flats and tasseled loafers, no nonsense meets a touch of flair. Rachel and Greg— Keds and Air Jordan. They shared mutual interests but were different enough to make life interesting. Tony and Gwen—cowboy boots and sling pumps— total opposites that immediately set off fireworks. It's all in the shoes."

Her sides pinched with laughter. "Please tell me you haven't shared this loony-tune idea with anyone."

"It works."

"So what would we say? We have a wide assortment of loafers? Or if you prefer the casual type, here's a list of Top-Siders." She whooped with laughter.

"Others read palms, tea leaves, horoscopes. I read soles. S-o-l-e-s."

"Oh, brother! We *are* in trouble. I bet I could come

up with a computer program that would work better than your shoe theory."

"No way." He crossed his arms over his chest, suddenly defensive. "Computers are too impersonal."

"Shoes are...that's just ludicrous," she countered.

He squared his jaw. "I'll take your bet. Let's see who can make the first soul mate match—my theory or your program."

"Deal." She had every confidence she'd win. Hands, er, feet down. "What's the prize?"

"A bigger share of the profits. Seems only fair."

"Sixty-forty split, then? Instead of our fifty-fifty now?"

He nodded. "Put your money where your mouth is."

She grinned. "Of course. Because I'm going to win."

ROUND ONE ended with Jack one and Jessie zero.

After the sign went up over their door, clients ambled, marched and ran inside searching for a soul mate. It was as if the name tapped into a societal need. Everyone, from gray-haired recent widows to bored married men to long-legged blond eye-catchers wanted to meet their soul mate. And they were willing to pay big bucks. But the thought of trying to find soul mates was more than daunting and had been keeping Jessie up late at night with pictures of penny loafers, high-tops and cowhide boots stomping through her mind. She had to admit, Jack had been right about the name. But it didn't mean his theory worked.

More determined than ever to win their bet, she flipped the switch on her computer, heard the familiar hum and watched the screen come to life. It gave her a sense of security. She'd come up with a rock-solid computer program, a questionnaire that would get to the heart and soul of their clients, rather than shoe size and heel preference. She'd find a logical way to match clients efficiently, precisely, permanently.

After all, weren't spouses as interchangeable as shoes? Seemed that way to her. At least, she'd watched stepmoms walk in and out of her life as if through a revolving door.

The bell above the front door at Sole Mates jangled. Another customer? Already they had ten signed up at a slightly discounted but highly lucrative price. And they'd only been in their office a week. At this rate, business would be a success long before Jessie had calculated.

Eager to greet a new client, Jessie made her way through the offices to the reception area. They still had work to do on the place, but it was taking shape. Next week, the new receptionist would start.

She rounded the last corner and her business smile turned to pleasure. "Oh, hi, Amber."

Dressed in a red power suit and carrying her sleek, court briefcase, the tall brunette kicked off her high-heeled pumps and gave a sigh of relief. "How's it going? People falling in love around here yet?"

Jessie grinned at her friend. "You better watch out." They'd first become friends in elementary school, neither having ever been "boy crazy." Over the years, they'd kept each other focused on following their dreams. "Long day in court?"

She nodded. "A stalking case." Rotating her neck and dumping her briefcase, Amber shrugged off her work as easily as her shoes. With barely a flip of her wrist, she tied her shoulder-length hair into a knot on top of her head. "Wanted to bring you something."

"Me, too, I hope." Stretching as if he'd just woken up from a nap, Jack sauntered into the room. He wore his usual faded jeans and a black T-shirt. Ever since he'd quit his lucrative job as national sales manager for a shoe company, he'd traded in his suits for jeans and bare feet. He looked as if he belonged on a beach, not downtown Dallas.

"Sure, I can share." Amber placed her briefcase on the desk and popped the brass tabs. "Have you read this? My latest client wrote it. It's the new rage." She pulled out a thick book with a bright red cover.

Jessie rolled her eyes. "Not again."

Jack chuckled. "See, I told you, baby sister."

"I'm not the baby," she insisted.

"By two full minutes."

"So you've read *Matched Souls*?" Amber interrupted.

"Oh, sure." She opened a desk drawer and showed her friend five more copies of the same book. "We've been inundated with requests because of that book."

"Just another theory on love," Jack said. "I could have my own book, if I had a Ph.D. after my name."

"Sure you could, Jack." Jessie patted his arm. She'd read Wade Brooks's bestseller...or at least tried. It had been a little ooey-gooey for her, like a sappy long-distance commercial.

"You watch, I'll prove my theory works."

"Not before my program kicks your butt." She sounded more sure than she felt.

"You better hurry, then. A couple I introduced last night just called. They're going out again tonight."

"Was that a slipper and a loafer?"

He sent her a smug grin. "How's your program coming?"

"Great," she lied. "Terrific. But mine isn't as iffy as yours. When I introduce the first couple they'll probably be off to Vegas to tie the knot that very night."

"Yeah, right." He smirked, setting her teeth on edge.

She had to admit, only to herself, that her program was handing out more problems than solutions. Dr. Brooks's book had given her hope. He'd written that everyone had a deep hole in their soul that needed to be filled by someone else. She'd tried to contact the love doctor to ask him questions, but she'd been rebuffed by both the publishing house and his agent. She'd never come close to reaching him. She needed answers from an expert, someone to guide her about love and soul mates. If she didn't hurry, Jack would win their bet before she even got her program up and running.

"What theory?" Amber asked.

"Let me explain," Jessie said, staring at her brother's tanned feet and Amber's stockinged ones. "You two make a great example! I never noticed it before but...but according to Jack's theory, you two are a perfect match!"

"What?" Amber's brown eyes widened and she curled her stockinged toes into the plush carpet.

Jack looked startled. "What are you talking about?"

"You both go barefoot. Why, I should have figured it out a long time ago. You two were made for each other. Let me input a questionnaire for both of you into the database to verify this."

"You're nuts," Jack said.

"That's absurd," Amber stated, squeezing her feet back into her sleek red pumps.

"You better leave the sole analysis to me, baby sister."

She shrugged off his comment and turned over a book. She stared at Dr. Wade Brooks's black and white photo. He looked serious, scholarly, knowledgeable. He hid deep-set eyes behind a pair of wire-framed glasses. He had a rugged jaw, sporting a dark five o'clock shadow, which hinted at an unconventional side. Maybe, just maybe, he was the answer to her problem.

He'd written about formulae and filling gaps in people's lives. If she could work his formulae into her program, she could figure out what was missing in her clients' lives and match them with their soul mates. Or at least someone who'd keep them company during the evenings.

Then she'd win that blasted bet with Jack.

"Amber," she said, "you know Dr. Brooks personally?"

"Yes. But he's not very sociable."

"I don't want to date him. I just want to talk to him."

"HERE COMES another one."

Wade Brooks slanted an irritated frown at his best friend Tom. "You can't distract me, Kendall." He shifted his attention back to the eighteenth hole. "Face it, I'm about to kick butt." He grinned, enjoying the rare moment. "And I mean yours."

He'd waited a long time to put Tom Kendall, one of the few men on the pro tour capable of beating Tiger Woods, in his place. It had taken four years of friendship, at roughly two rounds a week, which came to seven thousand, four hundred and eighty-eight holes, for Wade to reach this pinnacle of a moment. *Nothing* would distract him.

"You're finally going to be the one to buy me a beer."

Tom laughed. "Not if *she* gets here first. She's even got your book tucked under her arm." He gave a low whistle. "She's a looker. Not like the last one."

The "last one" Tom referred to had ambushed Wade at the ballpark. Out of self-defense, he'd left before the seventh-inning stretch. Recently he'd filed for a restraining order against another woman who had a penchant for looking in his windows.

His agent, with a bemused smile, referred to *them* as groupies. His mother, a whispered prayer on her lips, called *them* romantics. Wade simply called *them* desperate. They wanted what he'd experienced with Tanya. What they didn't understand was that that kind of love came along only once, if you were lucky, in a lifetime. He wished he'd never written that damn book.

"You know," Tom interrupted before Wade took a swing at the ball, "you ought to pay attention to this one."

"No, thanks."

"Hell, Brooks, you ought to go out with someone...anyone."

Wade's grip tightened on the putter. He didn't want to get into this. Hadn't he had this same conversation with his mother last week? Before that, his housekeeper had started in on him. "I'm thinking about it."

"Takes more than thinking." Tom's laugh disrupted the peace and serenity governing the lush rolling hills of the exclusive golf course. "Prepare yourself, Brooks, this woman is gonna knock you for a loop."

Not bothering to look in the direction Tom indicated, Wade grinned and waggled his club. As he shifted the steel putter toward the white dimpled ball, a pair of spiked heels digging into the short, manicured green turf entered Wade's peripheral vision. Against his will and better judgment, his gaze snapped to the seductive arch of an ankle and delicious curve of a silk-covered calf. His grip turned sweaty, slipping on the putter as it made contact. The ball shot to the side, missing by about four feet what would have been a birdie, and made Tom jump out of its path.

"Damn." Wade strangled the grip of his club and wanted to break it across his knee.

Women had crawled into his limo, followed him as if he were a celebrity, and had now tracked him down on the golf course. As a high school kid, he would have loved the attention. It was a red-blooded American male's dream come true. But reality tended to be less entertaining than pubescent fantasy. Next thing he knew, women would be staking out his bathroom.

Tom gave an aggravating chortle. Wisely, without a word, he positioned himself near his own ball and studied the easy shot that would tie the contest and make him the winner again.

"Wade Brooks?" the woman who stood a few feet away asked, her voice as smooth and sexy as her short, white linen skirt.

His anger heating to a slow boil, Wade slid his gaze up her body. He took his sweet time acknowledging her. It required every ounce of self-control, discipline and patience he'd acquired while working on his doctorate to bite back the sharp words clawing at his throat. He called on every psychiatric trick in the book from slow, deep breaths to counting to ten. Nothing extinguished the fire inside him. When ten didn't work, he tried eleven, twelve, but finally gave up.

With a last-ditch effort at suppressing his temper, he tried to look at the situation positively. Having lost to Tom once again, he could only think of one good point. His best friend had been right. She was a looker.

"Dr. Wade Brooks?" she asked again. She glanced down at the book she held. *Matched Souls* was his psychological study of love and romance. Flipping to the back cover picture the publishing house had insisted be used, she gave a succinct nod, as if answering her own question. "I've been trying to reach—"

"Look, lady—" his tone teetered between irritation and full-fledged anger "—if you want your book signed, you'll have to wait. I'll be doing an appearance in another week. Check the papers." Not only did he resent her intrusion, he wanted to blame her for all the past year's encroachments into his private life. "I'm in the middle of something here—"

"Brooks," Tom said, squatting beside his golf ball, "move out of my way." He grinned at the woman. "I'll be finished with the love doctor in a jiffy." He lined up his shot as if he were playing pool. "Then he'll be all yours."

"I can hardly wait."

A raspy, seductive quality had entered the woman's voice, having the same effect on Wade as a shot of tequila. She took a step to the side. A step that accentuated the lines of her sexy legs beneath her narrow skirt. A step that moved her closer to Wade. He caught a whiff of sultry perfume that he couldn't name and didn't want to.

Crossing his arms over his chest, he waited while Tom took an eternity to finish him off. The woman squinted against the afternoon sun, but her blue—no, green eyes were cool and assessing as they moved slowly over him. His body instinctively burned with awareness. Anger, he corrected. This woman had some nerve.

Tom took his shot and sunk the ball to win. Chuckling, he cracked his knuckles in a showmanship manner that raised Wade's hackles. "I'll be waiting in the clubhouse for my beer, Brooks." Tom looped his golf bag over his shoulder. "Good luck, lady."

Having no intention of hanging around, Wade turned on his heel, shoved the putter into his bag and stalked to his own cart.

"Hey, wait!" The woman followed him.

Wade could hear Tom laughing to himself as he maneuvered his golf cart down the narrow path. Cursing beneath his breath, Wade dropped his bag into the back of his cart and climbed into the driver's seat without giving the woman another glance.

"I didn't come here for an autograph," she said, her voice breathy as she tried to catch up. "Oh, damn!"

Releasing the brake, he shot her a look, smiling with satisfaction when he noticed her broken heel. She kicked off her pumps, gathering them up as she sprinted toward his cart.

Before he could put the cart into gear, she'd jumped into the passenger seat. "Mind giving me a lift to the clubhouse?" She gave him a subtle smile that transformed her mouth into a pouty invitation. "My heel broke."

Irritation shot through him. "Lady, you've already ruined my day. What more do you want?"

"Just a few minutes of your time." She settled her hands in her lap, drawing his attention to the slim curve of her thighs.

"I'm all out."

She crossed her legs, angling one toward him. He heard the whisper of her stockings, noticed the racy red shade of her painted toenails and smothered his sudden appreciation.

"I have a few questions for you," she said, her voice a honeyed tone that had his hands tightening on the steering wheel.

"Uh-huh." He'd heard them all, every proposition imaginable. Eager to get her out of his cart, and out of his life, he drove too fast over a speed bump, making her gasp and clutch his arm in an effort to stay in her seat.

A fissure of electricity ripped through him. Her fingers were cool and silky, but her grip was as strong as steel on his bare skin. Furious at himself for not getting away from her fast enough, he gave her a withering look.

Slowly her touch softened, gentled, and she smoothed her fingers along his skin, as if easing out the wrinkles she'd caused in his composure. But her light touch electrified him.

"Sorry," she muttered.

"You should be."

"I know this was probably a bad time." She had an intriguing face, not classically beautiful, but angular and pixielike at the same time. Interesting. Appealing. Riveting. And something about her seemed sincere. Somehow she didn't have the look of a crazed fan. She had sharp, assessing, intelligent eyes that intrigued him. That fact warned him away from her almost as much if not more than a lunatic fan chasing him. He fixed his gaze on the road and remembered the trouble she'd already caused.

"I was desperate."

Uh-huh. He'd figured that. Weren't they all?

"I've been trying to reach you for weeks."

Oh, great. A stalker. He pressed on the gas. Not much farther to the clubhouse. The gleaming white building shimmered in the sunlight at the top of the hill. Where was security when you needed it?

"Didn't Amber mention me?"

Was there one acquaintance or friend who hadn't tried to hook him up? He wasn't interested.

"Lady, I'm not in the mood for your little games. You just cost me—"

"I'll pay for the beer." She tugged on her short-cropped brown hair, which tried to hide her femininity but only revealed a slender, swanlike neck that made him think of Audrey Hepburn. "In fact, I'd like to buy you lunch or dinner. Whatever's convenient."

He bit back a growl. It wasn't the beer, dammit! And he didn't want to break bread with this woman. No matter how alluring her eyes...those eyes with their long, sweeping lashes were a mixture of misty green and tempting blue, sex and sin, all tangled into one aqua swirl.

"I'm booked." He turned into the first vacant parking spot and killed the engine. "Now leave me alone."

HOW COULD SHE LEAVE him alone? Just walk away and forget that he might have the very answers she needed? No way.

Jessie watched him stalk toward the clubhouse, his hands balled into fists, his pace clipped. He had cute buns, she noticed.

She shook her head at her crazy, erratic thought. Having seen his black-and-white glossy on the back of his book, she should have been better prepared. The photographer had failed to capture Wade Brooks's raw animal magnetism. Instead of a pale, lanky scholar, she'd found a tanned, virile man with broad shoulders, a trim waist and tanned, muscular legs. Even a color photo couldn't have readied her for the strength she'd felt touching his arm...or warned her of his firecracker temper.

Why had he gotten so irritated? Good grief! It wasn't her fault he'd missed his shot. She hadn't hollered out to him. She'd stayed on the periphery of the putting green. But as most men, he'd had to blame somebody for his own mistake.

"Round One," she whispered, climbing out of his golf cart. "I'm not done with you yet, Dr. Brooks."

He had the answers she needed to finish her questionnaire and computer program. Then she could put Jack's shoe theory in its rightful place. She wasn't about to lose this opportunity. Not when Jack was already so far ahead.

She worked her way across the hot pavement, feeling the sting on the bottom of her feet, her hose snagging on the graveled surface. Irritation setting in, she dangled the pair of pumps from her fingers, secured Wade's book under her arm, and entered the clubhouse.

When she reached the air-conditioned, swanky interior of the exclusive country club, she'd worked up a sweat in the Texas summer heat. Her makeup felt sticky and cloying, making her eyelashes feel heavy and her face like a Halloween mask. Her silk blouse stuck to the small of her back and her panty hose pinched her waist. She shouldn't have bothered dressing up for this elaborate ambush. Fatigues would have probably been a better outfit to catch Dr. Brooks. As frightful as she figured she must look, she wasn't about to retreat. Not when she had the psychologist pinpointed to one location.

Passing through the lounge, she waved at Amber, who'd given her an entrance pass to the club, but veered toward Wade's golfing opponent who sat alone at the bar. "I see Wade already bought your beer."

He gave her a salute with the long-neck bottle and a jaunty grin. "Struck out, eh?"

"I've only been up to bat once. The game's not over."

He gave her a wink. "With that attitude, darlin', you're not out of luck yet."

"Never." She stuck out her hand. "Jessie Hart."

"Tom—"

"I know, Mr. Kendall. The famous golf sensation." She smiled at his obvious pleasure that she'd recognized him. "Are you playing at the Byron Nelson Tournament next weekend?"

"Playing to win. You want to join me, sugar?" He leaned toward her. "I could use a good luck charm."

"I'm not the bracelet type."

Taking a swig of beer, he studied her for a moment. "Got your sights set on Wade, eh?"

She looked past Tom and scanned the lounge for the elusive author. "He's a tough one to get close to."

"That he is. Got a good-size chip on his shoulder. Think you can knock it off?"

Frankly, she didn't want to get *that* close. She simply wanted—needed to pick his Ph.D. brain. "Has he left?"

Tom signaled the bartender. "Let me get you a drink. Wade will be back after he's showered. I'll introduce you."

Yeah, right, she thought. As soon as Wade saw her in the lounge, he'd sneak out. In fact, he might have already left, which would put her back at square one. Not this time.

"Thanks, but I can handle the introduction myself."

Excusing herself, she slipped off the stool and headed toward a long hallway where she'd earlier noticed the men's locker rooms. A calculated, nervous glance over her shoulder confirmed the area was deserted. She hoped the dressing area would be, too...except for Dr. Brooks.

With a solidifying breath and a quick prayer that this would work, she darted inside the locker room. Her heart pounded. She wasn't the type to spring a trap on a man or to corner one in a dressing room. But desperate times called for desperate measures.

As she edged forward, moving like a cat burglar, she heard a man's low rumbling voice on the other side of a bank of mahogany lockers. It wasn't the famous psychologist. Another man laughed in response, making her flinch. Then footsteps, slow and plodding, and more than one pair, moved toward her. She zipped around a corner, her breath trapped in her throat.

No one appeared or hollered, "Hey, lady, what the hell are you doing in here?" No one blew a whistle and yelled for security. After a few uneasy seconds she heard the whoosh of the outer door closing, and sucked a breath into her tight lungs.

To her left, she could hear the spray of a shower. Was that Wade? Or some other unsuspecting male? She couldn't just barge in and find out. She shouldn't be here in the first place. If the doctor hadn't shunned her phone calls or been so difficult to track down, she wouldn't be about to do the unthinkable!

What would her mother say?

Actually, she'd probably be pleased. After all, hadn't her mother taught her to be dogged, determined, to never give up? Nina Simmons Hart wouldn't hesitate. She'd charge right in. Before it was too late.

But Jessie wasn't her mother. And her nerve began to wane. Her whole life she'd revered her mother, tried to emulate her. Now was the perfect opportunity to charge ahead.

The door to the locker room whooshed open. Panicking, she bolted forward, out of sight, and jogged down a tiled hallway. She glanced over her shoulder but breathed easier when she realized she was in an empty corridor. She turned around and stared at a row of shower stalls.

Silence echoed in her ears. Before she could budge one way or the other, some innocent man's arm reached out from the last curtained stall and grabbed the fluffy white towel hanging from a brass peg. Her knees started shaking, and she was actually grateful that she'd broken her heel and stood flat-footed.

The shower curtain rustled. Now what?

Oh, God, she thought, panic icing her veins. A hand shoved the curtain to the side and Jessie found herself staring, unable to blink or look away or act demure. She felt as if she'd been caught in the high beam of a headlight, frozen with fear or anticipation, she wasn't sure which. *Oh, God!*

Wade Brooks stepped out of the shower stall, his towel flung casually over his broad, tanned shoulder. His wet, black hair stuck up in all directions. He shook his head and water sprayed across the room. Water beads dotted his tanned broad shoulders in a chaotic and intoxicating manner. Even though he stood sideways, she could see the moisture glistening in the dark hair that covered his chest. Tiny rivulets ran down his body, over the flat planes of his stomach, the narrow curve of his back and the taut muscles of his buttocks.

Her breath caught. Heat flared inside her. *What have you done now, Jess?*

# 2

As Wade Brooks rubbed the towel over his face and head, he turned, walking slowly toward her. The slap of his bare feet against the damp tiles rang in the small, confined area. Jessie's face burned. She'd made a horrible mistake. But she couldn't move, couldn't run, couldn't think. She could only stare...at Wade Brooks...at *all* of Wade Brooks.

"What the hell?"

Her gaze collided with his steely blue one. Sparks skittered along her spine. Mortification didn't begin to describe her embarrassment. The air in the small passageway seemed to evaporate. Her heart beat its way into her throat. She coughed, sputtered. "I—I...Dr. Brooks."

*Look him in the eye!* Too aware of his sleek, sinewy, totally naked body, she glued her gaze to his. But every rational thought went down the drain. And she wished she would be sucked down, too. "W-what a surprise!"

He scowled, a look that sent both terror and intense awareness pumping through her veins.

"You're the one I—I needed to speak with." She'd hoped to sound casual, as if she'd run into him in an ordinary hallway, as if he were fully clothed, and her nerve intact, but her voice gave a telltale squeak. She clasped his book to her stomach, shifted from foot to foot and dropped one of her shoes. She left it, not willing to bend down...or to drop her gaze.

"What's next, lady?" He propped his fisted hands on his slim hips.

*Don't look down, Jessie. Just don't look below his waist.*

"Are you going to stake out my toilet next, hide under my bed?"

"N-no. Of course not." An inappropriate giggle bubbled out of her. She clamped her mouth into a firm line. *Oh, God, he's not covering himself with the towel. What do I do now?*

Perspiration broke out along her upper lip. "I d-didn't mean to intrude...to ruin your golf game earlier." *What are you saying? Don't apologize! And keep your eyes on his face!*

She focused on the lock of black hair falling across his proud forehead. Okay, she could admit she hadn't thought this through. What would her mother do? Nina certainly wouldn't perspire. She'd remain calm. She'd get to the point. But Jessie's thoughts blurred. "Or to d-disturb you during your shower. But I've tried more c-conventional ways of getting in touch with you. You're a hard man—"

Her gaze dipped to his very male, very naked... Snapping her attention back to his face, she felt heat burn its way through her.

He raised a cynical brow, but kept his frown intact.

"I mean, you're a difficult man—" Her throat tightened. *Good going, Jessie.* "Of course, you don't know me from Adam. Why should you return *my* calls? You probably get thousands. I can certainly understand your reluctance."

"No, you probably can't." His mouth cut a razor-sharp line across his face.

Her stomach twisted into a giant Girl Scout knot. She gestured toward the doorway behind her. "Let me buy you a beer."

He crossed his arms over his formidable chest; his frown made her knees weaken. "Say what you came to say and get it over with."

"Here?" She swallowed the thick lump in her throat.

"You chose the spot."

She had. She just hadn't anticipated he'd be naked during their discussion. "O-okay." She took a step backward and wished for a wall to lean against, something to support her. "I needed to ask you some questions about your book."

"Did you read it?"

"Yes."

"Read it again."

"Look," she said, her irritation getting the better of her. Why wouldn't he cover himself? What was he? An exhibitionist? "I didn't want to read your book. I thought it was a crock of—" She clamped her mouth shut and reined in her temper. "It had some interesting points that I'd like to ask you about. Even though I don't agree with all your ooey-gooey talk about love and romance. I live in the real world, not some fantasy.

"I don't buy that there's some great love, a soul mate, lurking around a corner, waiting for me...or you. It's the same old hogwash little girls have been fed for centuries with fairy tales of princes on white steeds. But no matter what I believe, my clients believe it. And at the moment, that's what's important. So, I've got to work around their naiveté."

His left eyebrow lifted and the corner of his mouth

pulled to one side. Her hand clenched into a fist. If he laughed at her, she'd give him a good hard punch to his very taut, very corded abs. *Keep your eyes on his, not on his gorgeous body!*

"Are you a psychologist?" he asked.

She blinked. "No."

Thankfully his towel covered what she'd been trying not to look at. "What are you?"

"A...a computer programmer."

He frowned. "What kind of clients do you have?"

Relief poured through her. Finally here was her chance! "My brother and I, we have a dating, er, matchmaking service called Sole Mates. As in s-o-l-e. But meaning s-o-u-l."

She saw the question in his eyes. "Don't ask. My brother's from L.A. Anyway, we'll have our grand opening in a month. But we already have a few clients. Several have brought in your book, highlighting the parts on soul mates. I'm trying to meet their expectations through my innovative computer program and I was hoping you could—"

He laughed then, a full, hearty robust sound that made his shoulders shake and the towel shift. A bulge beneath the terry cloth caught her gaze.

*Jessie Kathryn Hart, keep your eyes where they belong...on his!* His sapphire-blue eyes sparkled with mirth and it rankled her. She felt her spine stiffen with resentment. Then his grin faded, turning cold and hard, as if he was a statue. But from what she'd seen of him, he was not made of stone.

He jerked the towel off his arm and wrapped it snugly around his lean waist. She could only stare at his taut abdominal muscles rippling beneath his tanned skin, his narrow hips, the bulge beneath the towel's thickness. She forced her gaze upward. Too unnerved to look him in the eye, she stared at his Adam's apple, nestled along the sinews of his well-corded neck. She took a steadier breath and felt her confidence gain strength.

"You don't believe in love, romance, or soul mates." He rubbed the dark stubble across his chin, making a raspy sound that scraped the nerve endings along her spine. "Yet you're trying to set people up for life?"

"You don't understand."

"I think I do. You're like the old-fashioned charlatan, selling cough syrup out of your wagon. All for a buck."

Propping her hand on her hip, she puffed out an exasperated breath. "I think some people can fall in love. I've seen my brother hook up several of his friends over the years. They've all stayed married, happily or otherwise. He believes in red-hot passion. I believe in compatibility and mutual goals."

"In other words, love and romance are not for you."

She lifted her chin a notch and felt his disapproval all the way down to her toes. "Yes."

He remained silent. Uncomfortable with his insinuations, with his intense gaze dissecting her, scrutinizing her motives, she curled her toes into the coolness of the tile floor.

"Maybe you can explain to me what you meant on page one hundred and twenty when you talked about an unknown variable in a relationship." Her hands shook as she flipped through his book to the correct page. At least it gave her something to look at besides his very appealing, very masculine, very sexy body. Her fingers fumbled with the pages, and her brain felt as if it had congealed. She stared hard at the printed page, but none of the words made sense. "I'm trying to put together a questionnaire to be fed into my computer program. There can't be any unknown variables."

"Then you're dealing with the wrong kind of clientele."

She lifted her gaze, pinned it on his amused one. "What do you mean?"

"With all human relationships there are many variables working for and against it. The biggest, most volatile factor is the human heart. It's impossible to predict its reaction."

Or the reaction of other parts of the human body, she thought wryly, her gaze slipping briefly to his towel.

"Love's not an equation, Miss...?"

"Hart. Jessie Hart." She started to reach out to shake his hand, then thought better of it.

He nodded. "Miss Hart."

"Ms." It irritated her when people called her Miss, as if she were waiting to become a Mrs. And she wasn't. "I disagree. Love can be an equation. You state in your book that everyone is searching for something—love, security, whatever. And traits of another person, such as responsibility, wealth, even a Mother Hubbard personality, help fill the emptiness inside us.

"Not that I can relate. But if I can find the right questions to ask my clients, if I can figure out what it is they're really looking for, then..."

"Might as well start them in therapy. No one knows what they're looking for. We all kid ourselves, lie to ourselves, actually, that's why love requires an unknown variable. It's a well-known fact that most people date a certain type of individual, but marry the complete opposite. They know what they're looking for when they see it. It's called chemistry."

Chemistry! Jessie thought. Love had to be more. Didn't it? Not that she wanted to know—especially with such an arrogant man as Wade Brooks.

"Or is it simply the Old Boys' club, where men want to have their cake and eat it, too?" she asked.

"Are you always this irritating?" he asked, his gaze sharp.

"I've been called challenging." She tightened her hold on his book and switched the conversation off her. Again. "Men want all the perks of dating one type of woman, but then they wouldn't dream of taking that woman home to meet Momma. Right?"

"It's not a gender phenomenon. Women do it, too. You can't deny chemistry, can't predict it, can't force it."

She shook her head. "It's bull—" She stopped herself. "Baloney."

He gave her a fleeting smile. "Sounds like you have some issues with men to work out."

She squared her shoulders. "Give me a break, Doc. I don't need psychotherapy. I'm a realist. Plain and simple."

"Too bad." He rubbed a hand across his damp chest. "Because you're probably missing out on a few joys."

"I didn't come here to talk about myself."

He shrugged. "Good, then you'll leave me alone now, so I can get dressed." He cut his eyes toward her. "Or did you plan to spy on me some more?" He edged toward her, hooking his thumb under the edge of the towel tied securely at his waist. "What exactly did you want?"

"Help." Her voice squeaked and she took an involuntary step backward.

"With?" He came closer still.

She could smell the tangy scent of soap on his warm skin. Her stomach fluttered. Suddenly the tables had turned. She felt vulnerable, exposed, as if she were standing in front of him naked. Irritated at her response, she squared her shoulders. "My company, my computer program, of course."

"I don't think so. I think you came looking for something else." His intense gaze could not be ignored. She knew exactly what he was insinuating. But he was wrong!

Still, she felt her body respond to him, as a woman responded to the intimate touch of a man, but as she had never before responded to a man. The walls in the corridor seemed to close in on her. Her suit felt suddenly too tight, too constricting. But she wouldn't let this arrogant male get the better of her.

"You're the one living in a dreamworld, Dr. Brooks." She took a step toward him, her irritation getting the better of her. "You think every female in America is after you. Well, not me!"

"Uh-huh. Prove it." His voice was smooth but filled with a daring challenge. His arrogance skyrocketed her exasperation.

*Prove to him she didn't want him? Fine!* She took one more step forward, her gaze locked with his in a silent duel. In a rash move, she plucked away his towel, gave him a once-over, then a slow smile. Her insides shook, but she lifted her chin with defiance. "No, thanks, Doc. Doesn't do anything for me. Better luck next time."

She turned on her stockinged heel, but he caught her wrist and twirled her back around to face him.

"Not so fast." He hauled her against his bare chest and claimed her mouth.

Shock didn't begin to describe the sensations tumbling through her body. Her skin tightened, turned cold with outrage, then hot with desire. Through her clothes she felt his heat, the hard planes of his body, his maleness pressing against her. As if she'd lost complete control, or her sanity, she rose up on her toes and slanted her mouth more fully across his.

He had a softer mouth than she'd expected. The smooth texture combined with the roughness of his unshaven jaw unnerved her. She leaned into him, her knees melting like ice cream in the heat. Her world tipped and rolled.

Immediately she yanked herself back. *What the hell have you done, Jessie?* Her mother wouldn't have let any man affect her this way.

Her mouth burned from his touch. Her face flamed. Her body thrummed from the heat he generated. She'd proven the exact opposite of what she'd planned. And she'd ruined her chances of getting the love expert's help for her program.

*Damn, Jessie, why didn't you think this through?* That was the problem, though. Ever since she'd met Wade Brooks, she hadn't been able to think rationally. It was as if her brain had contracted a virus. But Wade Brooks hadn't affected her, she insisted to herself. He was simply a man. It had to be that damn bet with Jack that had her so disoriented.

Unsteady even on her stockinged feet, she lifted her chin haughtily. "If I really wanted you, Dr. Brooks, I wouldn't be able to walk out that door. But just watch me."

"I will."

She turned once more and walked toward the door. Her joints felt stiff and uneven. She felt his gaze burn into her backside.

"You have a helluva nice walk."

Pushing against the heavy door, her foot slipped on the tile, but she righted herself and grabbed the door frame. Once outside she sprinted for her car, her heart pounding in her chest.

WHAT THE HELL was he thinking?

Nothing. Absolutely nothing. Okay, maybe certain parts of his anatomy other than his brain had been making his decisions.

*What the hell had he done?*

Too much. And not enough. His insides felt as if they'd been knotted into a pretzel.

*What the hell should he do now?*

Stay completely away from Jessie Hart. She was one dangerous woman.

He was an intellectual. He had a Ph.D., for God's sake! Why had he let her get to him? Why had he acted like a Neanderthal?

Because she'd challenged him. She'd aggravated him. And dammit, he'd wanted to prove that she'd been as affected by him as he had by her. But he wasn't sure he'd proven anything—except that he knew how to behave like a jerk.

Slamming his locker closed, he yanked on the knot of his tie too hard and nearly choked himself. He stared into the mirror and half expected to see hair growing out his ears and sprouting on his face like a werewolf. Jessie Hart had stirred something inside him and he didn't like it.

He stalked out of the men's locker room. By the time he reached the lounge where Tom was waiting, his thoughts had drifted back to that brief but sizzling kiss.

"From the look on your face, Brooks, I'd say you won that round." Tom Kendall slid a bottle of beer toward Wade.

Not likely. Scowling, Wade plunked Jessie's shoe on the bar and hitched his hip onto the edge of the stool. He wasn't sure which intrigued him more—the fact that she'd left her shoe as a calling card or the kiss that would be permanently seared in his brain. He rubbed his jaw slowly, remembering the demanding softness of her mouth. She'd kissed him back, hadn't she? Maybe he *had* proven his point!

With that thought acting as a salve to his bruised ego, he took a slow swig of beer, hoping it would douse the fire she'd started in his belly. But the bitter brew didn't drown the sweet, intoxicating taste of her. "I thought I'd reached a point where I couldn't be surprised, then..."

"Some woman comes along," Tom finished for him, "and knocks your socks off, eh?"

"To say the least." Wade shook his head, still not quite believing what had taken place in the men's locker room. Frankly, he couldn't say he was shocked by Jessie's behavior. He should have anticipated it. After all, she'd found him on this exclusive golf course, tracking him down to the eighteenth hole. What floored him was his reaction to her, his blatant sexual response, his overwhelming desire to corner her and kiss her again. This time making it a long, slow, deep kiss.

He took another gulp of beer. It wasn't like him. He usually maintained a cool head in such situations. But not with *her*. With Jessie, he'd felt on the verge of explosion.

"To women," Tom said, tapping his beer bottle against Wade's. "And more surprises."

"No, thanks." That was exactly what he didn't need. "What's next?" Wade leaned his elbows against the bar. "Soon they'll be storming my bedroom, hiding under the bed."

"Or if you're lucky—" Tom waggled his eyebrows "—under the covers."

Wade's scowl deepened. "That's not what I'm looking for."

He'd married his soul mate and lost her in a tragic accident. He'd never find anyone like Tanya. Not that he wanted to. That kind of love came along once, not twice. And it hurt too damn much to contemplate falling in love like that again.

"What, then?" Tom asked. "Or do you have somebody in mind?"

"Not a particular lady." Certainly not Jessie Hart. "But I've been working on a list."

Tom gave him a skeptical glance. "A list? Of potential dates? Of women you want to go to bed with?"

"A list of criteria." Wade had been thinking about this for a long time now. Maybe this incident proved it was time to take action. Loneliness weighed heavily on him, closed in around him, especially at night. It had replaced the throbbing ache that had once been sadness.

He had no one to blame but himself. He'd become a

recluse from most of his friends while mourning the
loss of his wife. He'd worked long hours, concentrated
on getting his doctorate, then written his book, and
over the past two years, traveled extensively on publicity tours. He'd shunned any advances from women,
unwilling to open his heart to anyone again. But
now...he had all the material things he could want, all
the spare time he needed, and no one to share it with.
Maybe that's why he'd behaved the way he had with
Jessie. Maybe it was simply a symptom of something
missing in his life.

He wasn't looking for love. He didn't need or want
that kind of heartache again. He doubted he could
find it anyway. The love he'd shared with Tanya had
been once-in-a-lifetime. But he craved friendship,
companionship, with someone other than his golf pro
buddy. Obviously he needed a physical release.
Maybe he simply needed sex, as his friend so often
told him. Mindless sex, without commitment or ties.
But that wasn't his style. No, it would have to be in
some kind of a relationship. But it didn't have to be
ever-after, all-consuming love.

"You're saying," Tom interrupted his thoughts,
"criteria like long legs and big—"

"Not exactly." Wade couldn't hide a wry grin. He
rubbed his hand over the stubble along his jaw. "More
like what I'd like in a companion."

Tom crossed his arms over his chest. "A companion? You make a woman sound like a stuffed animal.
Or a good hound dog. Someone seen and not heard."
He chuckled. "Not a bad idea. Maybe I should have
thought of that before my first, second and third
wives."

"Takes more than thinking." Wade jabbed Tom's favorite phrase right back at him.

Tom picked up his bottle and took a long pull. "It's a damn good fantasy. So how does your latest fan—" he jerked his thumb over his shoulder "—fit into your criteria?"

Jessie Hart wasn't at all the kind of woman he wanted. She was dangerous to his peace of mind. She stirred things inside him. She made him burn for something more. It scared the hell out of him. He wanted a calm, soothing relationship. A partner. And Jessie made him feel as if he could lose control at any moment. "She doesn't."

"Too bad. Or maybe not. Did she leave her number? Maybe I'll look her up."

"Just this." He rolled over her shoe, the long, sloping heel fitting the contour of his palm as intimately as the curve of a woman's body, conjuring up sizzling images of her kiss.

"Cinderella, eh? Could be a fun fantasy date."

"Looking for wife number four, Kendall?"

Tom clapped him on the back. "Just a good time."

Why did that irritate him? He felt a twist in his gut that reminded him of jealousy. Ridiculous! He teetered between rational and irrational thoughts of Jessie. What had she done to him with just one kiss?

"And a good time," Tom added, "is exactly what you need because you've got those bachelor blues. Been there once or twice myself. Always got me in trouble, then divorce court."

Wade wasn't looking for trouble or even marriage. But he was tired of being alone. He needed someone who'd share quiet evenings with him, who'd listen to his problems, who wouldn't demand too much. He toyed with the sexy spiked-heel pump lying on the bar, closing his fist around its length as she'd closed her silken grasp around his libido. Where would he find the kind of woman he was looking for?

He doubted Tom knew any women that were demure and soft-spoken. They weren't the golf pro's type. Where would Wade find someone? He sure couldn't wait for her to find him. The women who sought him out were desperate, needy.

Immediately Jessie came to mind and a surge of heat shot through him. He revised his thinking. Instead of needy, she'd been determined. But she *had* wanted something from him, as had all the others.

Their conversation spun around his head, stirring up curiosity like a dust devil. He should forget her, get her out of his mind. But she seemed as determined to hound him in his thoughts as she had on the golf course and in the men's locker room.

As suddenly as Jessie had barged in on him, a crazy thought popped into his head. Maybe she could help him. Wasn't she starting a dating service? What was it called? Sole Mates? The name intrigued him. Hell, Jessie intrigued him. She was ambitious, energetic, driven. And dangerous.

Maybe she'd be the right one for him. Not as a date or a companion. But with her crazy scheme of a computer program she'd be determined enough to find him someone. Hadn't she said she believed in compatibility and mutual goals, not red-hot passion? Exactly what he wanted. Love couldn't be boiled down to a simple equation, but companionship might be a possibility. Maybe, just maybe, Jessie could find someone who fit *his* criteria.

It was worth taking a chance.

# 3

WADE FELT AS IDIOTIC as Prince Charming searching for Cinderella with Jessie's sexy, high-heeled pump in his possession. But, he reassured himself as he drove to the address of Sole Mates, he wasn't seeking her out for any romantic reasons.

*Liar!*

Okay, he wanted her to find him a companion. What was wrong with that? Nothing, except he felt the unmistakable heart-pounding anticipation of seeing her again. Not a good sign.

He'd had two days to contemplate his foolish speculation, forty-eight hours to recover from Jessie Hart's kiss, two thousand, eight hundred and eighty-eight minutes to change his mind. He'd be better off if he ignored the plaguing loneliness, tossed her shoe out the window and concentrated on his next book.

His agent had been calling him for months, asking when he was going to send in a new proposal. His editor was hounding him for his next megahit. Fans wrote him, wondering when he'd have another book out, if they weren't mailing him their underwear or proposing marriage.

With all those reasons pounding through his head, he continued heading straight for Jessie Hart—er, her office. He'd made an appointment and wouldn't back out now. Something pushed him, forced him to find out if she had something to offer him...that is, by means of helping him find a companion.

He drove toward her office nestled in the quaint part of Dallas known as Turtle Creek. It was a chic spot, cushioned between a hot new bookstore with a coffee bar and a designer boutique. By the number of Porsches and BMWs parked in the lot, he reasoned the clientele she sought were some of Dallas's wealthiest bachelors and debutantes. Not a bad market to pursue, he acknowledged. These wealthy elite citizens had the money and time to spend on foolish ventures, such as the search for love and romance. He, on the other hand, had no need to find his soul mate. A companion would do fine.

His own Infiniti fit snugly between two spit-polished convertibles. This might work to his advantage. After all, he reasoned as he exited his car, he didn't want someone to spend time with him for his wealth. He wanted a genuine friendship, an equal partnership.

Outside her building, a simple sign—Sole Mates—had been erected. Wondering if he'd made the biggest mistake of his life, he tightened his hold on Jessie's shoe, pushed open the shop door and heard the tiny, discreet jangle of a bell.

"Be right with you!" A husky, feminine voice he recognized called from a back room.

Immediately, his senses went on full alert. Maybe this was a mistake. Maybe he couldn't control or resist the attraction dragging him toward Jessie.

Before he could leave, she rounded a corner. She stopped in the doorway, her short hair mussed, her eyes widening.

"You!" Her tone sounded accusatory, her voice

brassy, irritating. She shoved her fingers through her hair, finger-combing it in place, tidying the short wisps behind her ear. "What do you want?"

"You left something behind." He held out her shoe and watched a red hue streak up her neck to splotch her high cheekbones.

She smoothed her hand down her silk blouse and narrow blue-gray skirt. Her legs seemed even longer, almost endless, even sexier than before. He had to force himself to not stare.

"Oh." She reached forward and took the shoe from him, her fingers brushing his, making acute awareness spark inside him. "Thanks. You didn't have to bring it all this way."

"I know. Didn't you get my message?"

"Message?"

*This was a mistake, a big mistake, Brooks. Back out while you can.* Unfortunately he was too honest and too desperate to back away. The thought of another lonely evening, one more dinner with only the ticking of a clock as company, kept him there. Problem was, he wanted to ask Jessie to spend the evening with him, not find him a date. But a date with another woman, even a Victoria Secret model, would be safer than spending time with Jessie.

"I made an appointment."

"You did?" Her blue-green eyes widened then narrowed with disbelief. "Why?"

Her bluntness made him smile. "Let's just say you made me curious the other day." To say the least! The memory of that heated exchange made his nerves simmer with a sudden charge of electricity.

"And here I thought I'd made you boiling mad."

"Have to admit I'm not used to having women

barge in on my showers." His confession made him
uneasy, anxious to forget she'd seen him without his
clothes. Usually when women had that claim to fame,
he could at least say the same about them. But this
time he felt cheated. He had no doubt Jessie would
look incredible without her clothes.

His mind conjured up red-hot images of her sexy
frame, her body leaning into him, her long legs wrapping around him, holding him tight. His blood
pumped fiercely. A tautness pulled at his insides and
jerked him out of his fantasy.

What was it about her? Women had been throwing
themselves at him since his book had hit the book-
shelves. Even before that he'd never lacked for feminine companionship. But he'd never had such a powerful reaction to a woman. Even to Tanya. Their love
had blossomed over a long, extended period of time,
awakening like a flower in spring.

*This isn't love, Brooks, it's lust.* A whole other ball
game. One he preferred not to play.

Maybe it was Jessie's confidence and dogged determination, mingled with her charming embarrassment,
that intrigued him. Sure, that's all it was! And he
could easily dismiss her, too, as easily as she'd walked
out of the locker room after their kiss. Couldn't he?

His gaze settled on her mouth for a moment too
long. He remembered the feel of her lips, the silky-
smooth texture, the urgency, her underlying need. Or
had it been his? He wondered what it would be like to
make love to her. She wouldn't be passive. She'd take
and give equally. Irritated at his reaction, at his way-
ward thoughts, he reminded himself of why he'd
come here.

Rocking back on his loafers, he locked his hands behind him. "Now that I'm dressed, I want to know more about your business."

"Why?" She gave him a wary look. "You said you made an appointment?"

He nodded. "Talked to some guy who said to drop by anytime today. I said I'd be here at ten. You didn't get the message?"

Her gaze shifted to the clock. The hands straddled the Roman numeral eleven. "You're certainly punctual. I'm sorry but you must have spoken to my brother. Jack doesn't make a very good secretary."

Disappointment sifted through him. "So is this a bad time?"

"No. I mean, not at all." She turned her shoe over in her hands, her fingers tracing the spiked heel, her fist closing around its length. "I'm confused. What do you want, Dr. Brooks?"

He couldn't help but watch as her fingers traced the same contours he had earlier. But he doubted she imagined what he had. "Call me Wade. You came to me. Remember?"

She nodded. "How could I forget?"

Nervously, she hooked a loose strand of walnut-brown hair behind one ear, revealing a modest, yet tasteful diamond stud earring. He wondered if a lover had given it to her, if it was a family heirloom, or if she'd bought it for herself. *Who cares, Brooks?*

He did.

"When's the grand opening?" he asked.

"One month away." The nervous flutter of her hand called his gaze to her long neck. His senses instantly zeroed in on her. As she edged closer, he noticed how gracefully she moved, despite her height, which came close to meeting his. At six foot two, he rarely met women who could look him in the eye without craning their necks. But the top of Jessie's head would fit neatly under his chin and her body would meld perfectly with his in a lovers' embrace. *Forget this nonsense, Brooks!*

Purposefully turning his attention to the reception area, he tried to ignore her carefree, peach fragrance that made him think of long, lazy summer days and warm, breezy nights. He stepped away, putting much-needed space between them, and pretended to notice a pastel painting on the far wall. Instead he was only too aware of her soft, rhythmic breathing, her nearness, the fiery kiss they'd shared.

"You already have some clients, right?" His voice seemed to echo in the confines of the reception area.

"Taking as many as we can get. Right now, we've got about twenty. But we're adding to our list every day. The response has been amazing."

Feeling steadier, he rubbed his jaw and faced her again. "There are many lonely people in the world." And he should know.

"So it seems." She crossed her arms at her waist and she tipped her head to the side, studying him. A tiny line creased the skin between her eyebrows, and he had an irrational urge to smooth it away. "That's probably why your book sold so well."

"No doubt about it. People are hungry for love. To be cherished. It struck a chord in the public."

"Which resonated in your wallet." She grinned and lifted her hand before he could respond with a sharp retort. "Don't get me wrong. I think it's great. It's what I'm hoping is going to make my business a success."

His brow furrowed. "How did you get interested in running a dating service?"

"We prefer 'matchmaking'." She sighed and sat on the arm of the white chenille love seat, her high-heeled pump dangling from her foot, distracting him, scrambling his thoughts as he imagined removing that shoe and running his hands up her shapely calf. "That's a good question. I guess you could say it's my brother's fault. You see, Jack's a natural."

"As a dating machine?"

She gave a soft chuckle. "That, too. What I meant was, a natural matchmaker. When we were in college, he'd introduce his girlfriends to fraternity brothers—"

"Wait a minute. Girlfriends? *His* girlfriends? Purposely?"

With an understanding smile, she nodded. "Jack has a good heart, but he knows his limitations. He doesn't want to hurt or mislead anybody. When he'd feel his relationship was getting too serious, he'd decide it was time to move on. So, instead of dumping a girl, he'd introduced her to someone else."

Wade studied her for a moment, weighed what she'd shared. He didn't detect any judgment in her tone, gestures or attitude. Instead she appeared energized as she talked about their potential gold mine. "And it worked?"

"Nine times out of ten. The girlfriend was delighted. The fraternity brother was on cloud nine. And Jack was off the hook."

Still caught off guard by her candor, Wade took a moment to digest the information. He was used to women playing games, disguising their true intentions, but Jessie was a straight shooter. She didn't take offense to her brother's actions or to his inability to commit. In fact, she seemed to applaud it. Then he remembered her thoughts on love and romance.

"So, Jack decided he could do this for a living?" he asked.

"That was my idea." She lifted her chin with pride and a beaming smile. "Once the couples he set up started getting married, they'd publicly thank Jack for his matchmaking skills, often making a toast at the wedding. His reputation spread. I used to kid him that women didn't want to date him for his good looks and charm but because it was rumored that if a woman dated him, he'd introduce her to her future husband."

Wade shook his head in disbelief. "And Jack agreed to your idea about the business?"

"Not at first. I admit, it took a little arm-twisting. He was actually doing quite well as a national sales manager for a well-known shoe manufacturer. But now he's all gung ho."

"But not about marriage?"

"Correct."

"So, your brother has the same aversion that you do to love and romance?"

"I wouldn't call it an aversion." Her long fingers clenched and unclenched, but she met his straightforward question with an unwavering gaze that unbalanced him. "Let's just say it's a life-style choice. We're realistic. We don't get all mushy over long-distance commercials. We don't cry at tragedies. Call it a healthy reluctance, sort of like not wanting to catch the flu."

"Interesting." He rubbed his chin, trying to figure out why this woman was so different from the women who'd chased him down at ball games and interrupted his dinners for autographs. A crazy thought occurred to him. Maybe Jessie could ease his loneliness. She didn't want love any more than he did.

"Why?" she asked. "Do you think all women want marriage?"

"Most."

She shuddered as if she'd suddenly caught a chill. Her shoulders squared, lifting her silk shirt, forcing his gaze to focus on the gentle sway of her breasts. "I'm not most women."

"So I've noticed," he said, taking a step toward her, feeling the temperature in the room double.

"Glad I could expand your horizons, Doc."

"Wade." Why was he so intrigued by this woman? Maybe because each time he thought he could pinpoint her "type" she surprised him. She most definitely was not like any other woman he'd ever met. Or was she too much like Tanya? That startled him. Scared the hell out of him, actually. She wasn't what he was looking for. Not at all. "You're right. Most women don't waltz into a men's locker room."

A sheepish smile escaped her. "I'm never going to live that down, am I?"

He chuckled, the anger from two days ago having already dispersed. "I can't help but be curious. After all, your new company is in the business of sending people down the aisle."

"No. Our company is in the business of introducing people to each other. What they do beyond that is their business. Or their problem."

"So why come to me? What did you want me to do?" he asked.

She looked up at him with those wide, sea-green eyes, a blue mist swirling inside them. "I'm not sure anymore. I'm not sure you can help."

Her words suddenly made him want to help her. *You're crazy!*

"I thought maybe you could help me with my equation. Take a look at the questionnaire for my clients. Offer suggestions. But I understand why you wouldn't want to help. You must think I'm nuts."

No. He was—for finding her, for liking her, for wanting her. What had he gotten himself into? *Forget her, Brooks. She's not your type.*

But she had a matchmaking service. Maybe *she* could help him. That kept him from walking out the door. Maybe some of her clients *were* his type—the type of woman he had room for in his life. Maybe...

Maybe he'd gone off the deep end, too.

"What would you say if I agreed to help?" he asked.

Her dark eyebrows shot upward beneath her wispy bangs. "Why would you do that?"

With his fingers, he combed his hair into place. "Maybe to ensure you don't pull this kind of prank again. Or maybe it's as easy as 'I have my own reasons.'"

Slowly she pushed to her feet and gestured toward the open door that led to the offices. "Come on back. I'll show you around. We haven't finished moving in. I've been unpacking boxes for days, hooking up my computer and getting things somewhat organized."

She gave him a smile to beat all smiles. The hair at the back of his neck stood on end, as if in warning that dangerous territory lay ahead. Ignoring his instincts, he followed her through a narrow passageway and down a long hallway. Half-open doors kept him glancing from side to side into empty rooms. A few had gleaming desks, but most were still filled with cardboard boxes.

"You're going to use all of these rooms?"

Turning and walking backward, she said, "We

want our clients to have their privacy as they fill out their wish lists or read over potential candidates' résumés."

"What about videos?" he asked, imagining the typical dating service.

"No. Not everyone feels comfortable in front of a video recorder, especially having to talk about themselves."

He grinned. "But some do."

She laughed, a husky tone that glued his attention to her as she paused at the entrance to one room. "I'll decorate the others like this, to promote a soothing effect. Going to a dating service has to be one of the most emotionally difficult and nerve-racking events in one's life. So, we want to make it as painless as possible."

"I take it you haven't been to a dating service." He doubted she needed help finding dates.

Her right eyebrow arched, dipping just under the edge of her bangs. "Why would I?"

"You've got all the dates you want then?"

She shrugged. "Enough to suit me."

For some inexplicable reason, he felt a surge of jealousy. Was she dating someone now? *What business is it of yours, Brooks?*

"Other women might be bored or frustrated or ready to settle down," she continued, "but I like my life the way it is. I don't need a man to make me feel complete."

Relief shot through him. It didn't sound as if she was involved. "Then I'd say you're a prime candidate."

Her gaze shifted toward him, her eyes widening,

the blue-green swirls deepening to an enchanting shade. "For what?"

*What exactly, Brooks? Not to date you. She is off-limits. Remember that!* "Sounds like you're at the perfect stage in your life to meet Mr. Right...or what others might call their soul mate. Didn't you read my book?"

"Yes, I read it." She gritted her teeth. "But I couldn't relate to it." She brushed her hands over her arms, and he noticed goose bumps dotting her tanned skin. "If I am a perfect candidate, then I've been one all my twenty-seven years. No Mr. Right has come along to change my mind about marriage. And he won't."

"Because you won't let him?"

She shook her head. "Because I don't need him."

Someone should shout, *Timber!* She'd fall. When she did, it would be hard. But it wouldn't be for him. Because he would *not* get involved with her.

HER NERVES ALREADY RAW, Jessie showed Wade into a narrow study. The mint-green room had a small desk and two overstuffed butterscotch-colored chairs. A seascape decorated the wall. She'd spent all yesterday working on this one room. She had to admit it had a calm, soothing quality—which she needed. Her pulse had been racing ever since *he* had arrived.

She resisted taking him into her own office. It seemed too intimate. He'd already tried to poke and prod into her personal life. She preferred to keep their relationship on a professional level, at least from this point forward. Which meant no more thinking about him naked. And no more kisses!

Why should that make her feel disappointed?

While he read through the questionnaire, flipping from one page to the next and then back to reread, she paced in front of the desk, trying to put mental blinders on herself, to ignore his very masculine presence. He filled the tiny room, his broad shoulders seeming even wider in the snug, blue shirt. She began to wish she'd taken him into her office, at least it would have offered more space. She wouldn't have had to breathe in his intriguing scent, which reminded her of wood smoke and cedar, illusive yet penetrating, like the man.

Her thoughts flipped back to the locker room when she'd seen *all* of him. Suddenly her clothes felt confining, the room steamy hot. Good God! What was wrong with her? She felt like a teen tossed into a room with Leonardo de Caprio. She had a sudden urge to launch herself at Wade, throw her arms around him and kiss him as she'd dreamed of doing for the past two days...and nights.

Jack's words haunted her. *Unmistakable, uncontrollable passion. When you can't think of anything else.*

Well, she could. And she would. Now.

She'd return when he finished looking over the questionnaire. Curiosity made her want to hover, to read each of his facial expressions as he studied the pages in front of him. But once again her gaze veered toward the dark chest hair peeking out of the V-neck of his knit shirt. Her mind instantly remembered the matting of hair covering his chest, the way tiny drops of water had nestled there, trickling down to—

"I'll be back."

He gave her a slow, curious glance. "What if I have a question?"

"Do you?" she snapped, more angry at herself than at him.

"Did you write these yourself?" He indicated the questions.

"Yes." Her nerves turned brittle, as if a cold blast whipped through her, freezing her confidence. Ever since she'd found him in her waiting room, she'd felt unsure, awkward, as if she were the one coming to a matchmaking service for the first time. He'd been the last person she'd expected to find in her offices. That he might actually help her had been too much to hope for after the way she'd ambushed him. Now that he was here, she worried what he'd say—if he'd laugh at her attempts, if he'd somehow prove her program couldn't work.

"If you wrote it, then you're the one I need."

Their gazes collided. Something in the air shifted, snapped, throbbed.

"Er...I mean, you're the one I need to pose any questions to." Again, he flipped back a page to reread a question.

Sinking back against the desk front, she waited. What was he thinking? He looked so intense. A shock of wavy black hair fell forward over his furrowed brow. His thumb idly tapped the chair arm.

Her mind churned up a wide assortment of humiliating scenarios. If he laughed, he wouldn't be the first. But he might tell her she was way off base. Or he could wad up her experiment—what had taken her an exhausting number of hours to research—and toss it in the wicker wastebasket. Her confidence crumpled with each passing second.

Finally, after almost thirty minutes of nail-biting silence, he looked up at her, his gaze intense and strong, his firm jaw squared and decisive.

"What did you think?" she asked, the question

bursting out of her. She wanted his advice, needed his expertise to make her program work. So she could win the wager.

"Very thorough."

Her gaze lifted to his, registered honesty. Her chest swelled with relief and pride. She took what seemed her first full breath since he'd arrived at her office. "Thank you."

He let a smile slip, curve his mouth in a provocative way that had her stomach twisting into a knot and her mind thinking of anything but the wager with Jack and her new business. A hormonal wave swelled inside her and she wanted to kiss him.

"I have to admit I'm impressed."

A flush of pure pleasure poured over her. Stunned, she sank into the chair beside Wade, his knee only a few inches from hers. Looking down, she noticed the crisp, straight-edged crease in his khakis. Instantly she remembered the deep tan on his legs and the paler shade above...

Shaking off her errant thoughts and the heat about to consume her, she stood and moved to the chair behind the desk, forced herself to concentrate on making this project work. "There has to be something that needs changing."

He rubbed his jaw thoughtfully, creating a rough sound of fingers grazing over coarse, shadowed beard. "Not necessarily."

She had the distinct impression from the heat of his gaze that he wasn't speaking about the questionnaire anymore. Her skin burned with need.

"You've done your homework. I could probably tinker with some of the wording...but I don't think that will change the outcome. Before you do anything else to it, I think you need to test it. Have you started?"

Maybe she'd been wrong. Maybe she'd projected her desire onto him. Damn. She sat back, disappointed yet relieved. "No, not yet. I wanted to be sure it was correct before—"

"I'd say you're ready for a guinea pig." He matched her posture, crossing his arms, stretching the knit material over his broad shoulders and calling her attention to his wide chest. She remembered all too clearly the way his chest looked, the chiseled muscles, the dusting of dark hair that tapered down—

*Stop! Quit thinking about how Wade looks naked!* She had to get him out of her mind. But how? What better way than to concentrate on her work? Before Jack beat her and won the wager. She couldn't let that happen. She'd always been extra thorough, a perfectionist. Now it was time to act. "Maybe you're right. Maybe it's time to put my theory to the test."

"Good. I'm glad you said that. Because I've got the perfect guinea pig for your experiment."

"You do?" She blinked with surprise.

"How about me?" Wade gave her an irresistible grin that made her insides tremble.

Her body suddenly felt on fire, every fiber burning, every nerve ending alive. Disbelieving she'd heard him correctly, she shook her head. Was Dr. Wade Brooks, *the* expert on love and romance, *the* most eligible bachelor in the United States, if not the world, asking *her*, Jessie Hart, entrepreneur extraordinaire, half owner of Sole Mates, to find him a date? A soul mate? A lifelong companion?

Call the *Dallas Morning News!* Or better yet, the *New York Times.* This was a groundbreaking event. This could, in one giant home run, catapult her business into the stratosphere.

She stared at him, unable to digest the cataclysmic turn of events. A stunning weight descended on her like a fog bank. It seemed mystical, as if fate had somehow stepped between them and pulled them together. For this business deal, of course.

What a wonderful recruiting device this could be! If word got out—and she'd make sure it spread faster than rumors of a worldwide computer virus—that Dr. Wade Brooks was using her matchmaking business to find himself a soul mate, then women would descend on their offices like shoppers swarming Bloomingdale's the day after Thanksgiving. If she managed to make a love match for the famous writer, that would bring in even more love-hungry customers. This was definitely a turn of events she hadn't anticipated. But it could be worth a mint if properly mined.

Wait a minute! Jerking back her runaway fantasy, she realized the full implications. Wade wanted a woman. A lover. A soul mate. But he wasn't asking *her* for a date. He was asking her to *find* him a date. Bitter disappointment rose inside her. She had been wrong. He wasn't interested in her, after all.

*That's good, Jessie. You don't need or want him, either. Remember what Mother always says—don't mix business with pleasure.* And Wade would be pure pleasure.

"What's all this talk about guinea pigs?" Her brother, wearing a wide smile, his usual jeans and button-down shirt, angled his athletic body into the small room. "This is a matchmaking service, Jess, not a zoo."

She expected relief to wash over her at Jack's intrusion. After all, she was much too aware of Wade Brooks and far too disappointed by his offer. But instead of helping to steady her breathing, she felt the sharp twist of annoyance at his intrusion. "When did you get here, Jack?"

"A few minutes ago. Didn't you hear the door?"

She shook her head. She'd been too intent on Wade, too worried, too engrossed for her own good.

"I'm Jack Hart," he said, shaking hands with Wade. "You the fellow that called the other day wanting an appointment?"

"Sure am."

"So, do we have a new client, Jess?" her brother asked.

Before she could reply, Wade answered. "Consultant. I'm Wade Brooks."

Jack's brow crinkled. "Where have I heard that name?"

"Look on your bookshelf, big brother," Jessie said. "He's the love doctor."

Jack grinned as if he'd just figured out a Hardy Boys whodunit. "So she finally tracked you down. No wonder you didn't want to meet with me." He sent Jessie an affectionate, brotherly wink. "He insisted on seeing only you, Jess."

More cynical now than optimistic about Wade's reasons, she eyed her sudden volunteer.

"You must be the famous matchmaker," Wade said.

"Or infamous." Jack gave his legendary smile again. "How'd she wrangle you into this?"

Jessie's gaze collided with Wade's. She felt the magnetic pull, saw humor give his eyes an intriguing glint. Her heart slammed on its brakes.

"You wouldn't believe it if I told you," Wade said.

"If it involved my sister, I would." Jack gave Wade

a friendly, conspiratorial wink. "You have to watch out for her."

"So I learned the hard way." Wade's gaze shifted toward Jessie.

Wary of his motives now more than ever, and irritated at the two men, Jessie clasped her hands together on the desktop.

"Never take her for granted," Jack added, making Jessie clench her teeth.

"Not a chance," Wade agreed. "She's not like other women."

Indignation burned her fuse until she thought she'd explode. "Okay, you two, that's enough. Get out of here, Jack. We've got work to do."

"Yeah?" He picked up Jessie's questionnaire. "What are y'all up to? Oh, Jessie's computer program." He chuckled. "Don't worry, baby sister. My theory is going to make us a success. Not some lame computer program. Sorry, but I'm going to win our bet."

"Don't count on it. I'm ready to start matching clients and it won't take me long to find the perfect pair."

"Uh-huh." Jack looked too smug for her peace of mind.

"I suggested she get a guinea pig," Wade said, rising and leaning against the desk. "But what's this about a bet?"

"It all started when I told Jessie about my theory."

"Theory?" Wade asked, glancing toward Jessie.

She rolled her eyes and waved her hand in the air dismissively. "You wouldn't believe me if I told you."

"I made a bet with my sister that my theory about how to match couples would beat out her computer program any day," Jack explained, "So, you two enjoy your experiment with guinea pigs. But, if you ask me, it's a waste of time." Jack's gaze narrowed on Jessie. "And don't get any crazy ideas, sis. I won't be your guinea pig. I'm not in the market. Remember?"

"I know. I know." Was her only option to work with Wade? To find him a date? When she wanted to be first in line to volunteer to go out with him? *Get real, Jess!* What was wrong with her?

"I've got an appointment myself. I'll see you later. Nice to meet you, Wade. Come around anytime. And if you're in the market for romance, give us a call. I bet we've got several ladies who'd be more than happy to go out with you." Jack gave a slight wave as he walked out the door.

"Were you serious about volunteering?" she asked, her nerves brittle. She hoped he was, because she could use his help. But another part of her—an irrational part—hoped he'd been kidding.

"Yes," he said as he reclaimed his seat in front of her desk.

Her enthusiasm deflated. Something was definitely wrong with her if she put desire over business. Maybe she'd been working too hard. "What's the catch?"

"There isn't one."

"What was all that bull you fed me about fate and soul mates and there's only one true love? Your book was all about the love of your life." She remembered his sloppy, sweet passages about his deceased wife with a sharp pang, how his wife had died in an automobile accident on the other side of the globe. She'd skimmed over the story, shifting uncomfortably in her seat, flipping to meatier text.

"I didn't say I wanted the wildly-in-love, happily-ever-after variety."

Rising from her chair, she laughed. "I never knew anyone that set out to find the heart-trampling kind."

He shook his head, wiping a wry smile from the corner of his mouth. "We're not communicating very well." He motioned toward the chair beside his. "Have a seat and let me explain."

"This has got to be good." She settled herself into the seat, careful not to brush against him. "Okay, explain what it is you want exactly."

His eyes darkened to the color of midnight, the pupils dilating, engulfing the brighter blue shade like dark sin sweeping out the last glimpses of light. Heat swelled inside her, making her skin feel too tight.

She had the distinct impression that he wanted her. She was certifiable! Hadn't he just asked her to find him a date? Yet his eyes devoured her like a starving man's. Or was it only her imagination, some insane need inside her rising to the surface?

Her body thrummed as she remembered their shared kiss, how she'd wanted to deepen it, how she'd wanted to run as far away from him as possible. And she had. She had the same urge to hightail it out of the office now. But this time she held her ground.

# 4

WADE FELT THE AIR PULSATE between them, the rhythm throbbing with vibrant warmth. His gaze shifted toward her full lower lip and he imagined what it would be like to kiss her, slowly this time. Her clothes advertised her lithe figure. She definitely had curves in all the right places. He imagined her against him, their bodies melding together in a fiery heat. A heady sensation, like a double shot of bourbon, burned inside him.

He gave himself a mental shake, as if he were a drunk trying to stir himself from an alcohol-induced stupor. He wasn't interested in Jessie Hart. She was *not* his type. She was too independent, too absorbed with her own interests, too...energetic—and way too distracting. How could he concentrate on his work with her nearby?

No, Jessie wasn't for him. But, damn, he wanted her.

"You're right," he said. "I don't believe in love potions or cupid's arrow. Or the foolish presumption that someone could match up two people for marriage and link soul mates. It's absurd. Two desperate souls searching, striving. They decide if there's potential by the time the first cocktail arrives. They demand love blossom in three quick dates.

"No." He gave a sigh of resignation. "Love needs

nurturing, time to grow. I do believe in chance en-
counters and fate. And in once-in-a-lifetime love."
He'd experienced that and the pain of losing it. This
time he'd focus on compatibility. That was all he
needed. "A love like that doesn't come around twice.
I'm not looking for undying love." He winced, the
words biting deeply into his conscience. "I simply
want a nice companion."

"A companion?" She stared at him as if he'd
sprouted antennae out the top of his head. "You
mean, like an escort service? If so, then you're knocking on the wrong door."

"That's not what I mean." His mouth thinned into a
straight, impenetrable line of defense.

"Then what?"

"A partner."

"For business? For writing?"

"More like a friend, a confidante, a...a..."

"A maid? Or maybe a good bartender?" She gave
him a tight smile as if toying with him. "Or just someone to pick up your socks, bring your slippers, hand
you a drink and put supper on the table?"

He scowled. Damn her. Damn him for opening this
Pandora's box. "I have a housekeeper. I can pick up
my own socks. I can get my own beer, thanks, and I
can make a damn good bowl of spaghetti." His blood
pressure shot through the ceiling. "I want a companion. I want to settle down." But he wouldn't give his
heart away again. He gripped the arms of the chair.
Self-recrimination burned in his gut. "What's wrong
with that?"

"You want a charm bracelet." Her eyes blazed with
indignation. Just as her father had with all five of his
wives.

"No. I want more than that. I'm not deluding myself that I can find another woman like Tanya, another soul mate. Frankly, if I could, I probably wouldn't choose that right now, either."

He clamped his jaw tight and forced his heart to stop thudding. With great effort, he pried his fingers off the armrests and flexed his hands.

He'd never expressed all of his pent-up feelings about his loss. He'd held the darkest ones inside, buried them deep but for some reason they'd popped up now like a cork in water. Guilt gnawed at him like a shark devouring its prey. He could imagine how he sounded—selfish, ungrateful, maybe a little daft, and totally disrespectful of Tanya's memory. Anger crept through him like a stalker, waiting for him, gauging his weaknesses. He should have kept his thoughts to himself. He felt stripped bare, just like the day Jessie had caught him in the locker room.

He'd loved his wife. As much as any man could love with his heart and soul, with every breath and thought. Nothing would ever change how he'd felt about Tanya. But he never wanted to feel that raw shredding of his soul again. The scars had not disappeared, but were embedded inside him, a reminder of all he'd had, and all he'd lost.

Aware of Jessie's steady gaze on him, studying him, analyzing him, he shifted in his chair. His clothes felt as if they'd shrunk on his body and constricted his every move. He tried to explain, to redeem himself. "It's not that I have anything against love."

"I hope not," Jessie chided. "It bought you a gorgeous house and paid for that country club membership."

Irritated at her flippant response in the face of the

burning pain that still resonated in his heart, he snapped, "I paid for it. I worked damn hard for it all. And I paid for love, too. In the most difficult way imaginable. But not again."

Damn, he'd said too much. Way too much.

Jessie's eyes widened, as if his words had slapped her. She reached for him.

Furious with himself, with her for stabbing a tender, sore area in his heart, he shoved back his chair and stood. "Look, I shouldn't have volunteered to help you. I don't know what I was thinking."

The air in the room thinned like fog over the water. He needed out. The pain burned like a red-hot coal in the pit of his stomach. He wanted to escape the anguish he'd suddenly unleashed, the rising guilt, and most of all, Jessie's curious aqua gaze that made his insides twist and turn with questions about the isolated life he'd created for himself.

"Good luck with your business." He flung the words over his shoulder and bolted for the door.

"Wait!" Jessie stood and grabbed his arm.

Her touch electrified him. She zapped his strength, his determination. Somehow, she reached that vulnerable, weak spot inside him that had been crying out for attention, for a human touch. The hairs along the back of his neck reared up.

He pulled her against him, felt every curve of her body, her very softness pressing into his need. "Forget what I said."

"I can't." She held on to him firmly, her hands cupping his shoulders, her fingers digging into him.

Without thinking, without hesitation, he dipped his head. Their breaths meshed first, then their lips melded. The kiss was insistent, greedy, urgent and wild. She fired a response in him that he couldn't resist.

Her lips tasted so sweet, their softness unraveled him. He wanted, needed more. She made him yearn for...hope for...

*No!* He couldn't accept that need, that weakness, or her strength. Reaching inside himself, he found the will to push her away.

"We shouldn't have done that." His voice sounded as tight and strained as his insides.

"I'm not going to apologize." She pressed her hand to his jaw, dabbed at the corner of his mouth. "Lipstick."

He knew. He'd tasted it, tasted her. And, dammit, he wanted more. Pushing back from her, he swore. "This was a bad idea from the start."

"I don't think so." Her jaw jutted forward. He'd seen that look before. A look that meant trouble. "You volunteered. And I can't—won't let you off that easily."

"I made a suggestion. You didn't seem too keen on the idea. Now I've changed my mind."

Her fingers curled into his arm with an equal urgency and a need he understood. She stared up at him, a pleading look making her gaze burn into him. "Forgive me for not sounding enthused. But I was confused—okay, concerned—about why you would want to be set up on a date."

"Isn't that what you're in business for?" he countered.

"Yes, but—"

"Do you question all your clients' motives?"

"No, just the really famous ones, the ones who've said matchmaking is a waste of time and money."

"I apologize for that." He hated to admit it even to himself, but he had respect for this spunky, feisty woman who could give as good as she could take. And heaven help him, he wanted to kiss her again, but this time never stop.

"Good." She shrugged one narrow shoulder and glanced down at her hand still on his arm. She kept it there and met his gaze squarely. "And I should ap—I shouldn't have pushed, questioned you so much. I shouldn't have kissed you, either."

Awareness of her warm fingers, her satiny-smooth skin touching his, muddled his thinking. Again, his gaze focused on her mouth. It could spit fire or soften like butter. It intrigued him, pulled him like a magnet. What was wrong with him?

"I may not be an expert in sex psych, but I started it," he said.

"And I'm ending it. It can't happen again. I don't make it a practice to kiss clients."

She could forget, put it behind her, that easily? He frowned, knowing he couldn't. "I'm not a client. I'm a consultant."

"Could have fooled me. Have a seat," she said, dismissing their kiss and the tension sizzling between them as easily as she might send back a too rare steak. She seemed oblivious to the effect she was having on him, her hand on his arm, the connection between them growing, building, burrowing into him. "You were about to tell me why you want me to set you up with a companion."

He stiffened. "I have my reasons."

"And I have mine for wanting you to stay and experience our first-rate service," she countered. "But my reasons are more obvious than yours. So share."

Her eyes met his solidly, honestly, gripping him in a gaze he couldn't escape and wasn't sure he wanted to. "I need to know more about what you want and why."

He wanted her. Plain, yet too complicated to comprehend. But she wasn't right for him. He needed someone who'd have a calming effect on him, not someone like Jessie who turned him inside out.

He took a shallow breath and felt his insides cave in defeat. He had to face it. Then maybe he could heal. "Because I'm alone."

He stared at the smoky-gray carpeted floor between them. For so long, loneliness had been a security blanket, comforting him over his loss of Tanya. But now, it was smothering him, like the guilt he felt for wanting to move on with his life.

But no one would let him. Each organization that asked him to speak wanted to know more about his relationship with his late wife, to peer like voyeurs into what little time they'd had together. Women who asked for his autograph always mentioned Tanya, and the love he'd written about in his book, how it had moved them to tears. No one would let him forget. And sometimes, that's all he wanted to do to make the aching pain go away.

"And I don't like it," he added, knowing he sounded petulant.

Immediately, her grip eased, then almost as quickly released him, as if they'd grown too close, too intimate. A line had been crossed. The damage done. He looked into her eyes then, needing a lifeline to return him to his sanity. The vibrant color of her eyes faded, gentled to the shade of a summer sky after a rainstorm. Was it pity? Concern? He wanted neither. But a part of him melted in the heat of her gaze, and he fought to rebuild the walls protecting his heart.

"I know what that's like," she said, her voice a mixture of silken empathy and chafing regret. "Look, I didn't mean to back you into a corner. Everyone who comes to a dating service has their own reasons. Being alone and not liking it is usually at the top of their lists."

"You came to me first, remember?"

Her cheeks glowed with awareness, the same blush she'd tried to veil in the locker room. "I pushed because I didn't want you to try to make a joke out of my business. How did I know you didn't want to use Sole Mates as an experiment for your next book on poor, pathetic souls who'd do anything to find love?"

"There's the idea I've been looking for," he said, needing a lighter moment to restore his bruised ego.

Her head jerked up, her eyes blazing. "You wouldn't."

"Lighten up, Jessie. I was only joking." He gave her a flirtatious wink that somehow made him feel younger, closer to his real age of thirty-one, when he usually felt a hundred and two. His smile broadened. "You started this. Pushed me toward the idea. But I've been mulling over the possibility for a while. It's something I've been needing but didn't want to admit."

"So, you will stay."

"Yes."

"You'll let me find you a…a companion?" Her smile faltered. She twisted her hands together. He wondered if she was as unsure of her computer program as he was. Her upper lip quirked as if it were a distasteful task he'd asked of her.

"No escorts, right?"

"Absolutely."

"Good, because I have plenty of women throwing themselves at me." The temperature in the room inched upward. All too easily, he remembered Jessie tracking him down. His overblown reaction to her had been obvious to both of them. Even now, he felt a tightness squeeze his lower belly. "If that's all I wanted, then I wouldn't need you..." He cleared his throat and tried to scatter the cobwebs in his brain. He'd need Jessie for a long time to come and it had nothing to do with business. But he had to draw the line the way she had. "I mean, your services."

This was his chance to change his mind, to run from his fears, his guilt, and Jessie. But he couldn't. He wasn't sure if Jessie's steel-blue gaze held him in place or if the time had simply come for him to face his own future...alone...head-on.

But was he alone? He sensed Jessie would do everything in her power to help him. Without condemnation. Without making fun of his decision. But would his desire for her interfere with their plan and her work? He had to get his libido under control.

"Okay," he said, and saw her hand tighten into a subtle fist of victory. "I'll let you *try* to find me a companion."

"That sounded like a challenge."

"Maybe it was."

"You're on, then."

His gut clenched in warning. "One condition."

"What's that?"

"No one can know about this."

"Excuse me?"

"There isn't to be one scrap of paper or one computer disk in this office with my name on it. If this were to get out, it could be detrimental to my career. There might be adverse publicity. I can't afford that."

"WHAT'S IN IT FOR ME?" She propped her hands on her hips. Wade Brooks as a client would bring in tons of women. And Wade Brooks's endorsement would guarantee the success of Sole Mates.

"You'll be able to tell if your system works. If you're asking the right questions on your questionnaire. If your computer program can make a match as easily as your brother seems to. You two have a bet riding on this, right?"

The bet. He could help her win, not only with his expertise and knowledge of the field—his desire to find a match was genuine and might prove easy to meet. Then she'd win.

Or would she?

Damn. It was the quintessential Catch 22. She wanted to find Wade a woman, but she also wanted to be *that* woman! What was wrong with her? She'd never been proprietary toward men. But then, she'd never desired a man the way she ached for Wade.

No, no, no! Her thoughts were topsy-turvy. His kiss had been far too potent. She had to get him out of her system—and fast. She needed a vaccine of some sort that would make her immune to him. Maybe finding him a companion would help her get over him, like a bad cold.

Taking as steady a breath as she could, she let the frustration ease out of her. He was right, of course, Sole Mates was reaping many rewards. She'd benefit most of all when she won her bet with Jack.

"You're right, Wade. I appreciate all of your help.

It'll be a tremendous benefit to my company and all of our clients." Maybe when she hooked him up with the right woman, he'd be so grateful he'd enthusiastically endorse her company. Obviously, he couldn't offer that blindly. She simply had to prove herself worthy. The same as she would prove her program could work as well as, if not better than, Jack's shoe theory. And she would!

"So, it's a deal." She stuck out her hand to shake his, a nonverbal agreement, a promise guaranteeing her silence and his help.

His larger hand engulfed hers, his warmth surrounding her, spreading up her arm and melting her insides like fired metal. Their gazes locked and held. Something sizzled between them. She wondered if she'd just made a pact with the devil himself, losing her soul...and her heart along with it.

"WHAT KIND OF CONSULTING is Wade Brooks doing for us?" Jack asked the next afternoon. "Is he going to give us an endorsement?"

"Uh, no, not exactly," Jessie hedged, now unable to reveal exactly what Wade's consulting would do for their company or to discuss her dilemma over setting him up with another woman. "He's helping me with the questionnaire for my program."

"I thought he said it was ready for a test run."

"Oh, yeah, uh..."

Jack picked her shoe up off the corner of her desk. Damn, she'd meant to take it home last night. It brought back too many red-hot memories of her first meeting with Wade, of his slick wet body, of his searing kiss. She gazed at the shoes as the images and sensations flooded back.

"Contemplating my theory?" Jack asked.

"Huh?"

"Why do you have a shoe here? Studying up to outdo me?"

"No. Wade dropped it by yesterday." She snapped her mouth closed. What had she insinuated?

"Really?" He lifted an eyebrow. "You wouldn't be hoping that your prince charming has the matching shoe, would you, sis?"

"I don't believe in prince charming." She wasn't and never had been the Cinderella type. Wade bringing back her shoe did fit the fairy tale. He just didn't fit her life. She shook off the strange sensation tightening her skin when she thought of Wade. She grabbed her shoe back from Jack and stuck it in a drawer. Out of sight, out of mind. *Yeah, right.*

"So, are you and the love doctor pussyfooting around? Is that how you got him in here?"

"No. Of course not." But the truth wasn't much better.

Jack had that knowing gleam in his eye. "Right."

"I'm not seeing Wade, except as a business associate. Strictly business."

Grinning, Jack winked. "Gotcha! Don't worry, sis, your secret is safe with me. I won't tell. It's about time you got a little...passion in your life."

"It's not what you think."

"Then what is it?" His challenging glare irritated her. Why did he have to know her so well?

Searching for a plausible explanation, her gaze landed on Wade's book. She'd thumbed through it again last night, this time more curious about the man than his theories on love. She'd felt as baffled by all the mushy emotionalism as she had before. Except she was beginning to relate to his description of the honeymoon phase of his marriage when he had trouble concentrating on clients and his studies.

She had trouble concentrating on anything but Wade. What did that mean? *Absolutely nothing!*

Her gaze shifted toward the clock. It was almost time for her appointment with Wade, which made her pulse accelerate at an alarming rate. *Nerves, that's all.* She wanted to succeed and she hated to be late for an appointment. She remembered Wade was punctual, too, definitely a Type-A personality. And two perfectionists could drive each other crazy—which meant they were totally incompatible.

Then the answer to Jack's question came to her. "Research." Of course! "He's doing research for his next book. He wants to keep it pretty hush-hush, if you know what I mean."

Jack gave a suggestive wink. "Right. Research."

"You do know what I mean, don't you?" she asked, praying Jack wouldn't say anything to anyone.

"It'll be a company secret." He glanced over his shoulder, then down the hallway. "Have you checked under your desk, in the closet? Any spies caught? What about Brandy?" Jack's eyes sparkled with humor.

"The receptionist? A spy? Give me a break. That would assume she could spell spy." The blonde could barely answer the phone and remember the name of their company. Jack had hired her. But then, Jack wasn't dating her for her brains. "How are you two doing?"

"You mean, has she walked me by an expensive

jeweler yet and gazed longingly at the diamond rings?"

Jessie grinned. "Something like that."

"Not yet. But it won't be long."

Then Jessie didn't have to worry about having Brandy as a receptionist much longer. The blonde would grow anxious, Jack uncomfortable, and he'd set her up with some friend. And bingo! Brandy would be off on a honeymoon in Tahiti. Then Jessie would get to hire the next receptionist. Maybe a blond male.

But amused blue eyes flashed in her mind. Along with thick, dark hair. And a body to write home about. She gave herself a mental shake. She couldn't—wouldn't think about Wade. Except as a client.

She tapped the stack of papers in front of her. This afternoon he'd fill out his own questionnaire. Then she'd input the information into the computer and give the data a spin to see if he matched up with any of their clients. Her jaw tightened.

She blamed her tension on Wade. On his returning to their office. On her spending time alone with him. Certainly *not* on any reluctance to set him up with a beautiful woman...another woman. After all, there was obvious chemistry between Wade and her. Definite chemistry. A virtual explosion each time they touched. And skyrockets when they kissed. But that's all it was—chemistry. And she could handle that.

Guilt wrapped around her throat like a noose. She'd never deceived her brother. It left a sour taste in her mouth. But she couldn't admit to him she was having explosive reactions to Wade. It didn't make sense. Jack would simply gloat. She had to keep her mind on business, on winning the bet. And off Wade.

"Ohmigod!" Brandy's breathy voice made Jack flinch and Jessie grip her pencil hard enough to break it in two. "*He's* here."

"Who?" Jack asked.

"Wade," Jessie answered. Immediately her hand went to her hair and she finger-combed a few wisps into place. "Send him on back."

Brandy pressed a hand to her heaving half-exposed breasts. "Have you read his book?"

"Have you?" Jessie asked, more surprised than if the receptionist had worn a skimpy bikini to work instead of her usual curve-hugging dress that looked as if it had been shrunk in the dryer.

"Well, no, but...well, I've heard about it...and I've seen *him* on TV. He was on the *Today Show* a while back. I thought he was good-looking then, but in real life he's...well, it's like meeting Tom Cruise. He's so charming. So incredibly sexy."

Jack looked more amused than irritated, and Jessie knew her brother was contemplating setting up their receptionist with Wade. Something sharp and way too uncomfortable stabbed at her. She had to put a stop to any such thinking. Before she could change the subject or divert Jack's thoughts, he said, "What's he wearing?"

"Wearing?" Brandy repeated. "Oh, this really yummy midnight-blue shirt that just matches his eyes."

"Shoes?" Jack asked. "What shoes?"

The bottled blonde blinked as if putting Wade's picture in her mind. "I don't know. Didn't get that far yet. But I'd love a chance to look him over some more."

"Never mind, you two. I don't want to leave our

cl—consultant waiting." Jessie plowed between Jack and Brandy, more irritated at her reactions concerning Wade than at either of them. "I'll show him in."

"COFFEE, TEA, ME?" The blonde giggled and batted her eyes suggestively. "I mean, milk?"

Wade had heard it all before. It didn't phase him anymore. But Jessie's deepening frown did.

"Nothing, Brandy," she said, dismissing the receptionist. "It's almost five. Why don't you call it quits for the day?"

"But what about—"

"I'll see to Dr. Brooks's needs," Jessie said in a clipped voice. Her gaze collided with Wade's.

Thinking of all sorts of possibilities—from a back rub to a foot massage to her arousing kiss, he gave her an amused smile. A flush stole up her neckline and stained her cheeks scarlet. His gut clenched.

Damn. Why was he here? To see Jessie? Or to find a companion? Definitely the latter. Even though he was focused on Jessie.

Jack cleared his throat. "G'night, Brandy. We'll see you tomorrow." Then he followed Wade into Jessie's office and closed the door on his confused receptionist. Chuckling, he said, "You'll have to excuse her, Wade, she gets a little enthusiastic."

"Doesn't bother me anymore. I've heard it all."

"I'm sure you have." Jack made himself at home in one of the armchairs and propped his bare feet on Jessie's desk. She gestured for Wade to take the other seat and started to walk behind her desk when Jack said, "So, tell me about this book you're writing."

"Uh." Jessie veered back around, almost bumping

into Wade. Her hand fluttered to his chest. His heart pounded. God, he wanted to kiss her.

"Need some time alone, kids?" Jack asked, amusement underlining his words.

"Wade," she said, removing her hand from his chest, "I had to explain to Jack that you're not really consulting for us."

"You did?" Apprehension sparked inside him. What if word spread? What if the news of why he was really coming to Sole Mates got out? "What did you tell him exactly?"

"That you're doing research for your next book."

"Research?" he asked, seeing the sparkle in her eyes as she explained her quick save.

"You know," she said, prodding him to agree, and stepping around the side of her desk. It put much-needed distance between them. "Why people are looking for love and how they're doing that these days."

"Oh." Relief shot through him. At least his secret was still safe. But he read the apprehension in Jessie's features as she waited for him to pick up the ball and continue their charade.

Clasping his hands behind his head, Jack added, "If you're interested I have my own theory on love and soul mates."

"Uh-huh," Wade said, hoping to encourage Jack to keep talking while he got his bearings, while he worked on forgetting what Jessie's hand had felt like against his chest. "Sure, I'd be interested."

"See," Jack said to Jessie, "I told you."

"You really shouldn't be sharing your theory, Jack."

"Are you worried someone will steal it?" Jack

asked. "If so, maybe I should write my own book. It's sort of like our secret-sauce recipe for our company."

"No, actually I'm scared someone will lock you up."

"This," Wade said, "I've got to hear." He plopped down in the extra chair and faced Jack. "Go ahead."

Straightening in his chair, Jack launched into his favorite subject. "My theory of how people can find their soul mates is—"

"Jack," Jessie warned.

"Shoes."

"Shoes?" Wade asked, confused.

"That's how I've matched lots of couples. By their shoes. You can really tell who will go together."

Jessie rolled her eyes and collapsed into her chair. "Now, we'll be on Jerry Springer's shoe—er, show."

Wade chuckled, crossed one ankle over his knee and rubbed the side of his leather shoe. "So what would you say goes with men's dress shoes? A stiletto type woman? Sandals? Platforms?"

Jack rubbed his jaw. "What are you talking? Lace-ups? Wingtips? Loafers?"

"Conservative toe caps."

"Ah, well, then a nice standard pump. With a three-inch heel. Enough to show off a pretty ankle, to turn a head, but not overtly sexual. Something like what Jessie wore the day she met you." Jack's eyes glinted with humor. "What'd you do with that shoe, Jess?"

Wade shifted his gaze between brother and sister, feeling as if he'd missed a family joke. And he was the punch line.

"You're not buying into this, are you, Wade?" Jessie asked.

"Makes sense." At least more sense than his own thoughts. "After all, shoes can express many aspects of a person's personality. Such as if they are laid-back or uptight. A perfectionist or a slob."

"She's a perfectionist, all right," Jack said. "But then, you probably already know that. She believes in compatibility, not passion. What about you, Wade?"

"Passion is for the young at heart," Wade answered.

"Passion is for any age. It'll make you young."

"Or old before your time," Wade replied.

"Hey," Jack said, "maybe you could use my theory in your next book."

"It's a possibility." He grinned at Jessie's annoyed expression. "Maybe I'll even call it Blue Suede Shoes."

"Or 'Bachelor Blues—How To Find The Shoe Of Your Dreams,'" Jack joked.

But Wade didn't laugh. The comment struck too close to his heart. He'd definitely experienced the bachelor blues. But he didn't want a fantasy woman like Jessie. Just a nice compatible one.

# 5

"ARE YOU SURE you're finished?" Jessie asked.

Wade bristled. "Positive."

"You must be the most thorough man I've ever met."

He handed her the questionnaire, unsure if her assessment was positive or negative. "I don't do anything halfway."

"Hmm." A suggestive tone entered her voice. Or was it his imagination?

Too aware that they were alone in the offices, Brandy having gone home hours earlier and Jack having left a short while ago, he felt the temperature in the room escalate. It gave him an odd sensation to be alone with Jessie again, making him nervous.

His gaze traced the neatly stacked books on the shelves in her office. A cluster of vivid flowers decorated the corner of her desk. He noticed a silver-framed photo of her and Jack, their smiles almost identical, whereas otherwise they seemed like complete opposites, from their coloring to their personalities to their views on love. Only their aversion to marriage seemed familial.

The sexy way her shoe dangled from the tip of her toe as she swung her foot back and forth caught his immediate attention. Inching upward, his gaze wandered slowly, longingly, across her arch, over to her bowed ankle and up along her silk-covered calf. Sudden heat made his collar too tight, too confining.

Somewhere in the corner of his mind, he wondered if some man, some lover, had sent those flowers to her, and, at the same time, he wished he could be that man. Irritation quickened his pulse. What did it matter to him if she was seeing someone or not? What possessed him to want her so desperately?

Maybe her aversion to matrimony attracted him. Of course! That explained the chemical explosions between them. She was unattainable, illusive, a mystery. Not to mention she had stunning eyes, knockout legs and a tempting mouth.

"Do you want to go over my answers?" he asked, somehow not ready to say good-night after he'd spent all day in her office. After all, they hadn't spent much time together. She'd hovered around him while he'd tried to answer the questions, until she'd driven him crazy with the subtle scent of her sensuous perfume. So he'd asked for privacy, then regretted the request.

Jessie rotated her neck and clicked off her computer. "It's getting late. I can go over them at home. If I have any questions, I can call you or—"

"What time is it?" Wade asked, feeling as if he'd entered a time capsule.

"Almost eight."

No wonder she'd said he was thorough. "Do you usually work this late?"

"Call me obsessive compulsive, Doc."

He chuckled. "Leave the diagnoses to me."

She sat forward in her chair. "Okay. What do you think?"

His gaze swept over her. A beautiful, sexy... dangerous woman. He cleared his suddenly constricted throat. "Someone extremely dedicated to her career. Someone who knows what she doesn't want...and what she wants...and goes after it. Without any excuses or doubts. Someone to be admired."

*But not someone to get involved with!*

"I don't know about the last." She looked uncomfortable with his assessment. "But the rest seems accurate. I am driven."

"Me, too." Releasing a pent-up breath, he said, "Now, I'm driven to find something to eat. I didn't intend to take so long on the questionnaire."

"Don't apologize." She met his gaze boldly. "You're a perfectionist."

"Habit from all the tests I've taken in school."

She gave a slight nod, slipped her foot all the way into her shoe, making his gut tighten confusingly, and then stood. Her skirt slipped down the length of her thigh and made him long to smooth his hand up— *Get a grip, Brooks!*

"Want to grab some dinner?" The idea was foolish, but he didn't regret it.

"Yes." She didn't hesitate or consult her calendar.

He didn't know if he should be excited or concerned. His biggest worry was aimed at his reasons for asking her to dinner. But looking into her blue—no, green, eyes, he no longer cared. "I know a great little Italian place not far from here."

In less than ten minutes they were seated at an intimate table for two in a dark, candlelit restaurant set in an old two-story home near downtown Dallas. The scent of oregano and garlic permeated the room. Wade ordered a bottle of Bordeaux and sat across from Jessie. Knowing her long legs were inches from him, he felt his body tighten with desire.

He wondered if he should be worried about some jealous boyfriend. He'd sensed she wasn't seeing anyone, but with her casual attitude about romance he could be wrong. Asking outright would voice his interest. Which he shouldn't be having anyway. After all, this combustible chemistry could be attributed to the enormous, vacant space in his social life.

Being with Jessie would help him feel more comfortable with a beautiful woman, so he wouldn't go overboard when Jessie introduced him to a companion. So, this was practice. *Yeah, right, Brooks!*

"Have you filled out one of those questionnaires?" he asked. Maybe her answer would tell him if she was dating anyone.

"No."

"Why don't you give it a whirl?"

She looked startled, as if he'd just asked her to walk the plank or jump off a cliff. "I'm not looking for a soul mate...or even a companion."

"So, does that mean you already have one?" He could have kicked himself.

"It doesn't imply anything."

That wasn't an answer. Certainly not a flat-out denial or confirmation. Frustrated, he leaned forward, his elbows resting on the corner of the linen-covered table.

"Are you seeing anyone now?" he asked point blank.

"Here's the wine," she said, shifting her gaze conveniently to the approaching waiter.

Frowning, Wade waited while the short, pear-shaped waiter uncorked the bottle, paused for Wade's approval, then poured the garnet-colored wine.

"Mmm, delicious," Jessie muttered.

Ready to pose his question to her again, he said, "So, are you or aren't you—"

"The first time I ever had red wine was when I was in college. I think Jack introduced me to it." She took a careful sip. "We were on a double date. I don't even remember who we were dating at the time. We were always trying to set each other up. It was sort of a joke between us."

If she wouldn't open up in one area of her life, Wade decided, then maybe she'd share another aspect. Curious about this woman, he said, "How come?"

"Jack and I didn't really know each other before college."

"Aren't you brother and sister?"

She nodded. "Twins actually. But we grew up separately. Our parents divorced when we were babies. The courts gave Jack to our dad to raise and I went to our mother. Jack grew up on the west coast, whereas I lived here in Dallas. We'd see each other occasionally at family reunions or in passing at the airport when I was going to my dad's for the summer and he was coming here. Kind of goofy, huh?"

"Divorce does strange things to families."

She took another sip of her wine. "Anyway, we both wanted to get to know each other better, so we chose the same college—Stanford. Gave us a chance to become acquainted. It's where we forged our friendship. But there was already a unique bond." She gave a husky chuckle. "It was funny how different and yet how connected we were. We made up for lost time by playing practical jokes on each other. Setting each other up with...well, not very attractive dates." She gave a full-throated laugh that had his gut tightening with raw desire. "I even set up Jack with a dog once."

Wade gave a polite smile. But his thoughts focused on kissing her again. Her mouth mesmerized him.

"A *real* dog," she added.

That caught his full attention. "This I have to hear."

"It was one of those Hollywood dogs. Jack waited for his date in the student center. She was supposed to carry a red rose." She wiped the corner of her eye and struggled to contain her laughter. "This standard-size poodle, with a diamond-studded collar and fuscia-painted nails, came prancing in, raised up on her hind legs and offered Jack the rose in her mouth."

He grinned. "What did he do?"

"Well, needless to say, all bets were off at that point. Then he hired this actor, a skinny little thing, to follow me all over campus like a love-starved—"

"Excuse me." A woman with shoulder-length sable hair, edged closer. She stared at Wade as though afraid if she blinked he'd disappear. "Are you *the* Wade Brooks, the author of *Matched Souls*?"

He gave a succinct nod. He'd been irritated at Jessie's intrusion on the golf course, but his reaction now went off the Richter scale. It took every ounce of restraint to politely say, "Would you like an autograph?"

"Oh! Would you mind?" She handed him a piece of paper and pen. "I just loved your book. I mean—" She pressed her hand against her heaving bosom. "It...you—" she gave him that suggestive look that always accompanied a hotel key in his pocket "—really spoke to me. On a very, deep, intimate level."

"Uh-huh." He scribbled his name.

The woman grabbed the paper and clutched his hand.

"Dr. Brooks is in a meeting." Irritation flashed in Jessie's suddenly emerald-green eyes.

Amused by her reaction, Wade hid a smile.

"He doesn't want to be rude but..." Jessie continued.

"I'm terribly sorry." The woman pulled a white business card from her cleavage. "Thank you."

After the woman dropped the card on their table and backed away, Wade said, "Thanks. Sometimes it's a little..."

"Awkward? Embarrassing? Stressful?" She gave an amused lift to her eyebrow. "Must be awful," she teased, "having so many women throw themselves at you. And you said you were lonely?"

Rankled by her humor, he snapped, "For your information, that is not the kind of woman I'm looking for."

He realized it wasn't until he'd met Jessie Hart that he'd been looking for a woman at all. Why did that unnerve him more than a complete stranger offering to take away his loneliness?

"Exactly what are you looking for?" Jessie asked, in a calming tone underlined with humor. "Her collagen lips? False eyelashes? Those expensive breasts? She certainly got her money's worth and knows how to, er, work them." Leaning forward, Jessie asked in a confidential tone, "How'd she get that card between them without even crinkling the corners?"

He couldn't hold back a laugh at that. "Must be talent."

"Hmm, I'd say."

Even from this distance, Wade could see the swish-

swish of the woman's ample hips as she wove her way through the narrow tables. Finding more humor in the situation because of Jessie, he asked, "What kind of shoes was she wearing?"

Jessie frowned. "Why?" Then a smile tugged at her generous mouth, reminding him of how wild and unguarded her kisses could be. Shaking her head, she said, "You're not going to try Jack's theory, are you?"

"Just a thought. It's got some merit."

"Give me a break. It's ludicrous." Jessie lifted the linen tablecloth and looked at Wade's shoes. He leaned over the edge, following her gaze, noticing the scuff mark on the toe of his casual loafers. Giving him a mischievous grin, she said, "Is that woman your type?"

*No, you are.* He shook loose that crazy thought. "I don't know. What's your assessment of my shoes?"

Her gaze slanted toward him, sparkling like a treasure trove of emeralds and sapphires in the candlelight. She gave him a suggestive smile that made his stomach nosedive. "You know what they say about big feet."

*WHAT HAS GOTTEN INTO YOU, Jessie?* Good gravy! She wasn't just flirting with the doctor of love. She was coming on to him!

It was the wine, she decided. Definitely the wine was making her tongue loose and her thoughts erotic. *No, Jess, it's Wade.*

They lingered over tiramisu and port...a mistake. She thought the wine had gone to her head. But the port nearly knocked her on her butt. She covered a discreet yawn with her hand and Wade signaled for the check.

"My treat," she said, reaching for her purse and the company credit card.

"No way."

"But you're a consultant," she protested, uncomfortable with him paying, as if it was a date or something.

"You're compensating me with..." He gave a friendly wink that made her wish it was a different kind of compensation. "Remember?"

How could she forget? She had to find him a companion. Why did that realization nettle her like a tiny thorn under her skin?

"I don't know why I'm suddenly so sleepy," she said, letting him place his hand at the small of her back as he escorted her toward the door.

"It's the wine," he said.

Or was it that she felt comfortable with Wade. Too comfortable. Too...too much.

"Maybe," she murmured. "I'm not used to wine. Guess I don't get out enough." Her cheeks reddened at her confession. Why couldn't she keep her mouth shut?

"Ah, so you're not seeing anyone."

She gave a slight frown. "I didn't say that."

"Okay, so you're dating somebody who's either out of town all the time or who's a tightwad."

"Maybe." She lifted her chin a notch, not understanding why she was playing this flirting game with Wade. What would her mother say? *He's a client and off-limits!*

"I'll drive you home," he offered.

Her nerve endings knocked together. "That's not necessary."

"My pleasure." He opened the door leading to the valet parking.

A flash of light blinded her for a second. "What's that?"

"Damn." Wade cursed beneath his breath. His shoulders bunched. Not again!

Jessie faltered, but he urged her outside, beneath the awning, in front of the crowd of photographers that had gathered to get a snapshot of him. Why couldn't they leave him alone?

Leaning close to her, catching a whiff of her alluring perfume that momentarily blurred his thoughts, he whispered into her ear, "Just follow my lead and I'll get us out of here."

While he casually handed the valet his ticket, the paparazzi fired questions at him.

"Are you two dating?"

"Who is *she*? The next Mrs. Brooks?"

"Is it true? Are you engaged?"

Like the flash of the shutters, he could see the headlines on the tabloids—Wade Brooks Finds His New Soul Mate. Or worse. What if Jessie got it into her head that this would be a perfect time for a little advertisement and announce Wade was consulting for Sole Mates? He couldn't allow that to happen. It wouldn't take long for a reporter to sniff out the truth. Wade Brooks Looks For Soul Mate At Dallas Dating Service. That headline would ruin his career. If not his life.

Lifting his voice above the din, he said, "We are not engaged. But—" he met Jessie's startled look and dared her to challenge what he was about to say "—we are dating."

Hey, she'd practically admitted she wasn't seeing

anyone. Why not him? It explained why they were out together. It solved a whole truckload of problems.

As the flashes of light clicked all around them, he ushered her into the passenger side of his car. He slammed her door and slid into the driver's seat. To prove his point to the photographers engulfing his car like a tidal wave, he pulled Jessie close, pressing her lithe frame against him, and did what he'd wanted to do all evening. He kissed her.

For the cameras, of course.

THE PORT had made her woozy, but the photographers and Wade's pronouncement was like a sobering combination of a cold shower and hot coffee. And his kiss had angered her.

Sort of.

Okay, her *reaction* to his kiss made her angry. How could two normal lips make her feel as if she'd been turned inside out? How could one simple kiss make her body yearn so desperately?

But it wasn't a *simple* kiss. It only complicated things even more. She'd had a hard enough time separating work from her crazy desire for Wade. This made it impossible!

"What the hell do you think you were doing back there?" she asked, her nerves raw. "What was that all about?"

"I'll explain in a minute." He zipped out of the parking lot and onto a main thoroughfare, leading them through downtown Dallas. He whipped his sports car around a big lumbering Cadillac and sped through a yellow light. "I have to make sure we're not being followed."

Her hand gripped the car door. "Does this happen to you all the time?"

"Not usually. But then I'm not usually out for dinner with...with someone like you."

Her lips thinned as he zigzagged through traffic. The engine roared in her ears. The leather seat vibrated with suppressed energy. Her body thrummed with desire.

Wade looked in the rearview mirror at the cars behind them, then downshifted and slowed to the pace of traffic. He gave her a surreptitious glance.

"What's that supposed to mean?" she asked, bristling at his earlier comment. "'Someone like me?'"

He laughed at her irritation and defensiveness. "I usually eat with the likes of Tom Kendall. It was bound to stir things up when I took a beautiful woman to a romantic restaurant."

"Beautiful?" she echoed, her mind dazed with confusion over the kiss and his compliment.

He shifted gears, making the tendons in his forearm contract, making her want to smooth her hand over the fine hairs and warm skin. "I apologize for all of that commotion back there. And for telling them we're dating. But chances are you'll be some mysterious woman—"

"Until my picture hits the papers."

"That's why I kissed you."

"So my mother would call to ask who I'm dating? Why I'm not being discreet?"

He grinned. "No, so they'd print the kiss, where your face would be obscured."

Why didn't that bring any comfort? And why did she want Wade to have kissed her for normal reasons, such as lust, desire, love. No, not love. Lust was fine with her.

"This is getting too complicated." Her heart thumped assertively against her breastbone. And she knew it wasn't because of the paparazzi. It was Wade's fault. "Now everyone is going to think we're dating, including my brother. I'll never hear the end of it."

But the truth was, she wanted to date Wade. That's what baffled, terrified, vexed her.

"It's very simple." He flexed his hands. Something inside her coiled tight. "Our dating will explain my reasons for being at your offices without raising questions that neither of us can answer."

But what would explain her desire to go on kissing him? She wasn't sure she wanted the answer to that question.

Would it be so awful, she wondered, for people to think she was dating the most eligible bachelor in America? Her insides twisted into a French knot. Maybe not. Or maybe it would be terrible, because only she and Wade would know the truth—that it was a charade. Why did that bring a sharp pang of disappointment?

"What happens when I try to set you up with a companion and she thinks you're dating me?"

He sighed. "I don't know. I hadn't thought about that. Maybe we'll give your client the same explanation you gave Jack. That I'm doing research on my next book. So I can meet with the woman, ask her questions, determine if I see possibilities, then move from there."

Jealousy surged like a bottle rocket inside her. How

could she set him up with someone else? It might prove to be the toughest thing she'd ever done.

Leaning back into the warmth of the leather seat, she stretched out her legs as she gave Wade directions to her house. "I guess I don't understand why you want a companion and not a soul mate. Do you think there's only one soul mate for you? And you're willing to settle for less?"

He gave her a steady, penetrating look before he shifted his gaze back to the highway. "I don't know anymore."

His silence vibrated inside the car as he followed the route to her home. When he pulled into her driveway and cut the engine, he leaned back into his seat with a sigh. "I've been confused lately."

She could relate.

He gripped the steering wheel with both hands, his knuckles turning white in the moonlight. "But I don't want to meet another soul mate. It hurt too damn much the first time."

She remained silent, but she felt her breathing turn shallow, her heart pound with sympathy, understanding and longing. She'd never loved someone the way he'd loved his wife. Maybe it was what sold romance novels, but it wasn't for her. Or was it? For the first time she felt as if she'd missed out on something vital, life-affirming.

"Tanya was strong, independent." He shot Jessie a look, then focused on the headlights shining on her garage door. He flipped a switch and darkness swallowed them. "Of course, you know all this since you read my book."

Skimmed, she clarified in her mind. "Hearing you

say it gives it more meaning." She reached for the door handle. She needed air. Space. Her freedom.

He put a hand on her arm and electricity skittered along her nerve endings. "Wait. Let me get it for you."

She looked over her shoulder, meeting his gaze. She could kiss him if she wanted to. And she did. But what would it mean? Where would it take her?

"I'll get your door," he said, his voice hoarse. He came around the front of his car and opened her door. Offering his hand, he helped her out of the low-slung sports vehicle, a car not made for short skirts or long legs.

Awkwardly, she tugged on her hem. She felt her skin ignite with an uncomfortable heat, sensing him behind her, even though he wasn't touching her. She heard his footsteps against the concrete walk. When she turned at her door to offer a hasty good-night, she felt her heart leap. He was close. So very close.

Her hand automatically came up between them and settled against his chest. She could feel the thudding of his heart, racing almost as fast as her own. She couldn't decide if she wanted to push him away or pull him closer.

"Would you like to come in for some coffee?" she murmured.

"Sure." But the way he was staring at her mouth told her he wasn't thinking of decaf or caffeinated. He was thinking of the kisses they'd shared. Wild kisses. Demanding kisses. Kisses that challenged, confronted, dared her. And kisses meant to cover a lie. But this time, she wanted Wade's kiss. One silent and meaningful. One that gave instead of took. And she knew she was in serious trouble.

Her hands trembled as she opened her door. She

flicked on the hall light and walked straight for the kitchen without a backward glance. But she knew he followed. She could smell his subtle, intoxicating scent.

"Decaf?" she asked.

"Doesn't matter to me." He settled himself onto one of the wicker stools at her counter.

She plopped a filter into the coffeemaker and tried to get her thoughts off Wade. Off the way he made her feel. "You were talking about your wife...your late wife."

He gave a slight shrug, as if uncomfortable revisiting that topic. "There's not much else to say. I loved her deeply, completely, holding nothing back."

Jessie wondered how it would feel to have someone love her that way. Cozy? Comforting? Confining, she decided. Definitely confining.

"I accepted her ambition," Wade said, "as she accepted mine. As we accepted each other. We gave each other room to grow. To paraphrase the old saying, I let what I loved fly away like a butterfly, to spread her wings."

Her spine stiffened. "'Let'?"

He nodded, sure of himself, of his love, of the past. "When I should have insisted what she was doing was too dangerous. I should have made her stay home."

The force of his words pounded inside Jessie. An odd mixture of uneasiness and irritation nettled her. Hadn't her father clipped her mother's wings? Only their divorce had set her free to pursue her abilities and talents in the business world. And Nina had succeeded.

"We didn't have a perfect marriage," he said before Jessie could explain how her parents' relationship had

suffered from such a belief. "From this distance, looking back into our past, I can see that now. I couldn't
see it as I wrote my dissertation, which became my
book. Our relationship was flawed from the outset,
because we didn't have a unified goal."

The deep, reverberating pain in his voice touched
Jessie, surprising her, pulling the carpet out from under her earlier annoyance.

"We had separate dreams. That, maybe more than
her death, pulled us apart." Stark pain shone in his
eyes, pinched the corners of his mouth.

In spite of her silent criticism that he'd wanted to
curb his wife's ambitions to suit him, Jessie was affected by his raw emotions. Setting the plastic filter on
the counter, she walked over to him and touched his
arm. She felt the tension in his muscles, the heat of him
pulling her closer.

*Watch out, Jess.* She felt way too much for Wade. The
intensity of her feelings unnerved her. But she
couldn't pull away.

Part of her wanted to ease his sorrow by setting him
up with a companion for life. Part of her wanted to
take him in her arms and hold him close, make him
forget the past, his pain, his wife.

"It's not an easy thing to do, lose someone you
love," he said, his voice rough with emotion.

She'd never realized what she'd lost as a child
through her parents' divorce. What you never had,
you never missed. But when she'd rediscovered her
brother, formed a bond with him, she knew she could
never give up his friendship. And she wasn't sure she
could ever walk away from Wade.

It was a crazy, irrational thought. She hadn't known
Wade long enough. She didn't want someone in her

life, consuming her thoughts. But she wanted Wade. There was no denying that.

Unable to stop herself, she looped her arm across his shoulders. His gaze magnetized her. Her compassion smouldered into something more.

He stared at her.

She stared back.

Caught.

But the trap was of her own making. And there was only one thing to do—run.

# 6

WADE WASN'T ABOUT to let her get away. He closed the space between them, pulled her close, until their lips were only a breath apart. For the first time in years, he felt alive. Really alive. His pulse thrummed. His skin burned with awareness and need. All because of Jessie. He couldn't seem to get enough of her. He couldn't get close enough.

Bracketing her waist with his hands, he pulled her onto his lap. He met her startled gaze and took advantage of her mouth opening with a gasp. He sealed his mouth to hers, kissing her hard and fast, sucking the air right out of her. Beneath his insistent pressure, her lips parted and he swept his tongue over hers, dipping and delving deeper.

Desire fired his blood. He could so easily lose himself inside her. With her in his arms, her mouth against his, he could forget his pain, his fears, his reservations. Like a starved man gorging on a succulent meal, he devoured her, tasting, touching, filling his senses, overloading his libido.

He clutched her to him. He wanted her, but more than that, he needed her. She consumed his thoughts, his actions, made him yearn and long for what he hadn't experienced in far too long—connection. They were so different, yet exactly the same. Both hungry, starving for more in their lives.

Jessie's stunned response shifted, turning around on him. Her arms circled his neck, her fingers sifting through the hair at his nape. Her kiss became frenzied, urgent, mindless. Her hands fluttered across his shoulders, tugged at the opening of his shirt, as if she, too, couldn't get enough.

Each breath was ragged. Each kiss desperate. Each touch as if it might be their last. If this continued, it would all be over too soon. But he wanted it to last and last and last.

Grabbing her wrists, he placed her arms behind her back, held her still, cuffing both of her hands with his one. He met her wild gaze. "Easy." He smoothed his hand down her throat, stroking her, feeling the heated desire rising from her skin. "You've seen me. Now, it's my turn."

Her eyes turned dark, as if the black pupils had swallowed the swirling colors of blue and green. Her mouth softened like warmed butter. Gently he cupped her jaw, rubbing his thumb along the soft underside. A tremor rocked through her. With barely held restraint, he slid his palm along her neckline, easing his fingers inside the top of her blouse, until the clasped button just above her breasts stopped his progress. Her skin felt hot, silky, he felt as though he were sliding into a creamy bath.

With slow deliberation, he unfastened the top button, then the next and the next. Her chest rose and fell in the frantic rhythm of his heartbeat. Easing back the panels of her shirt, he watched as the cool air from the vent above them made her nipples pucker beneath the white, filmy lace. With a sigh of pleasure, she arched her neck, leaning back, giving him free access.

His heart pounded, his hand shook with suppressed desire. He traced the contours of her throat, reveling in the smoothness, her heat. Gliding downward, he explored her chest and tested the satin edges covering her breasts. Pulling her toward him, he placed his open mouth against her fragrant skin, tasting her, feeling her heart thud and her breath catch. Heat shot through him, coiled inside him, tightened his groin.

"You're beautiful," he whispered with awe.

She clutched his shoulders, her short nails digging into him. He cupped one breast, molded her flesh into his palms, grazed his thumb over the dark, nubby center.

"We shouldn't be doing this." Her voice was deep, thready.

"I know."

But he couldn't stop. He didn't want to stop. Obviously, from her sultry looks and gasps of pleasure, Jessie didn't want to, either.

He found the catch nestled in her cleavage and snapped it open. The satin and lace cups drifted to her sides, framing her breasts. He touched her warm, bare flesh as he'd wanted to ever since the day he'd met her. As he flicked his tongue over one taut peak, he heard her ragged breathing loud in his ears. Or was it his own?

Placing his hand against her long leg, he felt her heat almost melt the silk hose beneath his palm. Slowly, erotically, he moved his hand beneath her skirt, along the inside of her thigh. His heart jackhammered with need. His body tightened with desire. He needed release. He needed her. Only her.

"Wade," she whispered, a wild hunger making her voice hoarse.

She felt her breasts tighten. A feathering sensation between her thighs banished all rational thought. Each touch, each kiss, each ragged breath seemed magnified, explosive. Never had she felt so desperate, so out of control. Her body ruled her mind. She'd fantasized about kissing him, having him touch her. She'd spent more hours thinking of Wade than any man. This moment, the culmination of desire, overwhelmed her. She wanted to lead him to her bedroom, wanted to feel him inside her, to love him all night. She wanted to wake up in his arms...

Then what? Heaven help her! What then?

*Don't think, Jess! Don't analyze. Live for the moment.*

But panic seized her. She blinked, feeling dazed, confused. How had they gone from an innocent dinner to groping to almost making love? What had she done?

*It's the wine. Definitely the wine.* But she knew the truth. She couldn't lie to herself anymore. It was Wade. It had always been Wade. And that scared the hell out of her.

"Wade." Her hand pressed against his chest. Her elbow straightened, pushing him away from her.

"What? What's wrong?" His vision was glazed in confusion.

It was the hardest thing Jessie had ever done. She wanted—needed him. But he wasn't right for her. It was a mistake. A big mistake.

She wasn't looking for love. She didn't want a man in her life right now. She didn't want Wade.

"I can't do this. I—I..." Her mind raced as her body yearned for his touch. She met his heated gaze and knew how much he wanted her, too. But that's all it was. Want. Lust. And for some strange reason, she realized that wasn't enough.

Frightened by her own needs, she stood on wobbly legs. She felt weak, her limbs fluid. But her mind was sharp, the edges of doubt pressing into her conscience. He wasn't the type of man who could have a fast, hot relationship, a weekend tryst, a wild affair. He was the type that loved...deeply, completely.

He'd never love the way he'd loved his wife. And she wasn't the kind to settle for second place.

She didn't analyze why that brought a sharp pang of regret. Instead she focused on him wanting a charm bracelet, a companion, a woman he could control. And that wasn't her.

"Are you seeing someone?" he asked. "Is that it?"

"No." The flirting was over. She had to regain her composure. Turning slightly away from him, she fastened her bra and hastily buttoned her shirt. She had to put a professional distance between her and Wade. "I'm not seeing anyone."

"Then what?" Irritation sharpened his voice.

"You're a consultant, a client. We shouldn't have...I shouldn't have let it go this far." She crossed her arms over her chest, still feeling his mouth on her, her nipples still crested with need, the ribbon of desire still pulled taut inside her. "You should leave."

He watched her for a long moment. "I'm not the kind of man who does this sort of thing casually."

"I know."

He ran his hands down the tops of his thighs as if trying to regain control of himself. He pressed his fingers into his knees. "You do strange things to me."

She swallowed the desire to ask him to stay. She

gripped her elbows, refusing to give in to this insanity. "Wade..."

"Okay. I'm going."

Standing, he turned, then changed his mind and came toward her. Alarm arrowed through her. If he kissed her again, if he gave her another chance, her resolve would crumble.

Tenderly he cupped her jaw. His gentle fingers sent shock waves down her spine. "I wouldn't hurt you, Jessie."

She gave a slight nod. He wouldn't *mean* to hurt her.

"You don't have to be afraid of me."

"I'm not." But she was. Afraid of what he did to her, the way he made her react and respond. Or maybe she was afraid of herself, the way she felt in his arms. She'd never felt such passion, never been consumed by it, never known she was capable.

He pressed his mouth to hers, a flutter of a kiss, a soft reminder of what could be. Her heart contracted with regret. "Good night, Jessie. You know this isn't over."

She took a step back, shielding her emotions with distance, and jerked her chin defiantly. "Of course not. I'll call you when I've input your answers into the computer...when I have a match for you."

"You can still do that...after...?"

"That was our agreement." She needed his help. Matching him with the right woman would help her forget Wade. Permanently.

If not, then at least she'd win the bet with Jack.

His jaw hardened. "I see. Always work first. Your career first." He gave a grim nod, the lines bracketing his mouth deepening. "Fine."

"A CONSULTANT, HUH?" Jack stood in her office doorway, a wide grin on his face. He held up the tabloid. A blurry black-and-white photo glared at her, reminded her of the roller coaster evening with Wade, his sizzling kisses, her tumultuous emotions, ranging from overwhelming desire to utter confusion.

She gave a nonchalant wave of her hand. "Oh, that."

Jack arched an eyebrow. "'Oh, that'?" He studied the photograph. "Looks like more than 'oh, that,' to me. It says here that—"

"I know what it says." Several friends and clients had called already to read her the article. She didn't need a recap from her brother. Irritation sharpened the pain at her temple. She'd had a roaring headache all morning, due to the wine last night. Not Wade. Or the way he made her feel.

*Yeah, right, Jess. Go on believing that one.*

"Explain to me again, because I'm a little fuzzy on this point, exactly what kind of consulting good ol' Wade Brooks is doing around here."

"I told you he's doing research for his next book."

"Ah," he chuckled, "so that's what this kiss is. Research."

"Jack," she said, her temper rising, "if you're here to harass me, I'm not in the mood. I have one helluva headache. And a lot of work to do."

"Yeah?" he asked, taking notice of the stacks of papers on her desk—the questionnaires she'd begun having their clients answer. "Need me to do something?"

She shuffled the papers in front of her, covering Wade's questionnaire. "No, thanks. I can handle it."

He tucked the newspaper under his arm and walked toward her desk. "What are you doing?"

Her heart pounded. "Setting up the financial records." She punched several keys on her computer until a different software program popped onto the screen, one that demonstrated a spreadsheet on their financial situation, in case he took a closer look. "You want to take over?"

"Not particularly."

"Knock, knock." A familiar voice made Jessie look over Jack's shoulder. Her brother turned away from her.

Jessie waved toward their guest. "Hi, Mother." She sounded enthusiastic, but all she could feel was guilt. How disappointed her mother would be if she knew how she'd let pleasure override common sense. Not again. Not with Wade.

A tall brunette in a cobalt-blue business suit strode into Jessie's office with the same confidence and aplomb she carried into the bank over which she presided. "You two should train your receptionist better. She sent me back without even an introduction."

"Mother," Jack said, bending to place a kiss on her cheek.

Nina grabbed the newspaper from under Jack's arm and slapped it onto Jessie's desk. Her carefully plucked eyebrow lifted in that dramatic way that revealed her disappointment. "I see you're aware of this."

Jessie leaned back in her leather chair and groaned.

Jack laughed. "I was just getting to the bottom of it."

Leveling her discerning gaze on her daughter, Nina said, "So, what's the story?"

"Nothing. It's all a misunderstanding."

"What do you mean?" Nina's brow furrowed. "The photographers weren't supposed to catch you kissing? Or Wade Brooks wasn't supposed to be kissing you?"

"Leave it to Mother to get right to the heart of the matter." Jack rubbed his hand over his jaw, erasing his smile.

"Both," Jessie answered, flustered, confused, exasperated. Why couldn't everyone leave her alone? Everyone, including Wade! She shook her head. "Neither. I mean..." What did she mean? "It was a joke. See, we were having dinner—"

"Was it a date?" Nina asked, her tone blunt.

"No. Business."

"Oh?" There went that eyebrow again. "You're not mixing business with pleasure, are you? I taught you better—"

"No, Mother, I'm not." Not anymore, anyway.

"Good." Nina placed her briefcase on the floor and sat on the edge of Jessie's desk. "So was it a ploy to drum up business?" A wry smile tugged at her mother's carefully painted mouth. "Not a bad idea. Who wouldn't want to come to Sole Mates now? Especially after seeing that one of the owners is able to make her own love match. And with such a handsome, wealthy bachelor."

*Please, don't remind me!*

"Is that what this was about?" Jack asked.

"I taught you well, Jess," Nina added, pleased with her new interpretation of the situation.

Guilt coiled inside Jessie. She wanted to confess that what Jack had predicted had occurred. She couldn't quit thinking about a man. She wanted advice, sympathy, a cure. She didn't warrant admiration. She'd failed miserably. Her confusing emotions surrounded her, cutting her off from her family and Wade.

"That's not what happened, either," she confessed, unable to accept her mother's praise. She shoved her fingers through her hair. Her temples throbbed. "You see—"

"Wade Brooks is consulting for us," Jack explained.

"He's doing research on his next book," Jessie countered. "And we couldn't reveal the real reason for us going out to dinner. So he made something up on the spur of the moment."

Both her mother and brother were silent for a few drawn out seconds, as if they didn't believe her.

"It's the truth," she added, wishing it was nothing but.

Her mother's mouth twisted with doubt and suspicion.

"Sure. Right." Jack gave her a broad wink.

Oh, what did it matter if they believed her? She wasn't dating Wade. But she wanted to!

"Well, be careful, Jess," her mother said, using her corporate tone. "Remember discretion. It's not smart business-wise to make a production of your private life."

How many times had she heard this particular lecture? Her mother had to be made of steel. She couldn't imagine Nina succumbing to the heat of the moment. Feeling the effects of defeat, she said, "I know, Mother."

"At least you got a good plug for Sole Mates in the paper."

Jessie nodded. Her mother could always see the potential in a situation and make it a positive career move. "We've already had several potential clients call this morning. I've got the afternoon slotted with meetings."

That's when she would try out her questionnaire on a few more unsuspecting women who might be Wade's new companion. Why couldn't she set Wade up with someone and be done with it? Her stomach twisted into a string of knots.

"So this—" she waved her hand toward the tabloid, trying to forget her headache, her jealousy, her pain "—hasn't hurt business one bit."

"Hey, Jess," Jack interrupted, "be careful of Wade. I think he could be your type. He might be the one to send you down the aisle."

His statement irked her. Couldn't he leave that topic alone? Wade was not her type. Yes, he made her hot and bothered, but that didn't mean they were compatible. "You don't have to worry about me. I'm not getting married."

"I wouldn't want you to get hurt."

"Wade can't hurt me." No man could. "I told you, we're not involved." But she knew their lives were much more entangled than she wanted them to be.

Nina glanced at her son. "Have you met this Wade? Why do you say he's her type?"

Jack nodded. "His shoes."

"You're kidding!" Jessie laughed. "That should prove the opposite. He wears golf shoes and Top-Siders!"

Nina rolled her eyes. "Not that shoe theory again. Are you still relying on that?"

"It works." Jack defended his theory. "I still have someone I want you to meet, Mother."

Nina stood abruptly and reached for her briefcase. "No, thank you." Settling her manicured hands on her narrow hips, Nina shifted her gaze between her two children. "I hope you've got more substance to this business than shoe types."

"Don't worry, Mother," Jessie reassured her. She'd prove her program worked by setting Wade up with his "type." Then she'd win that bet with Jack. Her mother would have plenty to be proud of then.

"I'm not worrying. I raised you right, Jess. You're too smart to listen to such nonsense."

Was she? The truth resonated like a gong inside her. She was in deep, deep trouble.

"WOMAN TROUBLE?" Tom asked.

Wade missed the chip shot. Sand sprayed like a fountain around him and the golf ball sunk lower in its hole. He cursed. Wade stood in the sand trap. He'd already knocked a ball into the trees and three in the water. What was wrong with him today? He knew the answer. Jessie.

"Having problems?" Tom hooked his club under his arm and waited for Wade to dig himself out of his latest trouble.

But what would work for the way he felt about Jessie?

"If someone would have some respect and refrain from talking, then maybe I could concentrate." He tried the chip shot again. This time the ball soared out of the trap and landed on the green with a dull thud.

"So, what's her name?" Tom asked.

Ignoring him, Wade climbed out of the sand, feeling the grit between his teeth and covering his legs. Once again, for the umpteenth time today, he cursed.

"You haven't been hiding somebody from me, have you?" Tom grinned. "Why don't we knock off and go get a beer? Then you can tell me all about your woman troubles."

"I'm not giving up."

"I've already got you beat, Brooks."

"Don't get so cocky, Kendall. We're only on the ninth hole." The way the day was going he'd set a world record for the worst outing in golf history.

Tom chuckled. "So, is it the one in the paper? The one you were kissing?"

Here we go.

"Wasn't she the one that bushwhacked you on the eighteenth hole last week?"

Wade lined up his shot. He squinted against the bright sunlight. The ninth hole looked as if it were a mile away. "Instead of bothering me, you could move on to the next hole."

Tom shook his head. "Wouldn't be polite. And as you know golf is a polite game."

Ignoring him, Wade swung and watched his ball sail through the air, falling shorter than he would have liked.

"So, this woman...this Jessie—what's her last name?"

"Hart," Wade snapped between his clenched teeth.

"I remember her. She's some looker. Did she meet your list of criteria? Was she a good companion? Obedient? Demure?"

"I wouldn't say that." Hell, she was far from what he wanted. Yet she'd invaded his thoughts, his sleep, his every waking moment. If he closed his eyes, he could remember her soft, alluring fragrance, her warm, sparkling eyes, her sizzling kiss. Damn.

It didn't matter. None of it mattered. He wasn't going to pursue her. She'd made it clear she wasn't inter-

ested. Frankly, she was way too headstrong, determined, career-minded. She didn't want to be a
companion. She didn't want love, either. And he
didn't want her.

*Yeah, right, Brooks!*

She was going to set him up with a date...a companion. And he'd be fine with whomever she found. As
long as it wasn't Jessie.

PRETTY. EASYGOING. In a prep school sort of way. In
fact, with her long blond hair tied back into a ponytail,
a cardigan sweater knotted around her shoulders,
candidate number six looked young enough to have
just graduated. Jessie glanced again at the woman's
application. Age, twenty-four. Not too young, not too
old. Just right, Jessie assessed.

She read the woman's name again. Missy. Even her
name sounded like a companion's. Grinding her back
teeth, Jessie withheld judgment until later—when
she'd input the woman's questionnaire into the computer's database.

"Well, Missy, Sole Mates is glad to have you
aboard. We'll begin working on finding you a companion as soon as possible."

"A companion?" Her squeaky voice was one strike
against her. "I want love, romance, a husband. Not
something casual and temporary. I want what Dr.
Brooks talks about in his book."

"Oh, yes. Of course." Jessie refrained from asking
Missy directly if she'd like to have Wade Brooks. What
woman wouldn't want him? She gave herself a mental
shake. *She* didn't want him. It was fine with her that he
wasn't her type. That he was the Top-Sider and golf

shoe type, while she was the corporate pump type. "Sole Mates will do its best."

"Is there a guarantee?" Missy asked, pulling her credit card from her purse.

"A guarantee to find your soul mate?" Jessie frowned. Was this woman for real? What was Jessie, God? "I'm afraid we can't make promises like that, Missy. But we will try our hardest. And with the plan you chose, you are guaranteed thirty-six meets."

She pursed her lips. "Will I get to meet your brother, Jack?"

"Possibly. But I'm afraid he won't be one of your dates. We have a strict policy at Sole Mates to avoid mixing business with pleasure." And she'd do well to remember that the next time she saw Wade.

Missy gave a nonchalant wave of her hand. "Oh, I didn't want an introduction to him per se. I wanted him to set me up with my potential soul mate. Sarah Wiles said that's how she met her husband, Ron. Sarah said Jack had some theory about matching people up."

Jessie nodded, having heard it all before. She clasped her hands tightly together. Her computer program would do a thorough job, too. "You are certainly welcome to make an appointment with Jack for his insights. Now—"

"Good. I'll take care of that on my way out."

"Fine." Jessie gave a tight smile and walked the woman to the door. "The receptionist will be happy to take your payment."

She watched Missy walk down the hallway, then closed the door to her office.

Missy was not Wade's type. No way! Trouble was,

she was beginning to think no one was Wade's kind of woman.

Except her.

*That's dangerous thinking, Jess.* She had better things to do than to dream about Wade, his devastating smile, the sound of his laughter when he let loose, and his unraveling kiss.

To prove he meant nothing to her, she returned to her desk, set the program to start and clicked enter. She heard the faint whir of the computer as it generated the data she'd already input. Then at the bottom of the screen, a match appeared.

Her heart lurched. Of course it wouldn't be her. She hadn't filled out a questionnaire. She wasn't that stupid.

Shrugging off the uncomfortable emotions tightening her throat and chest, she picked up the phone and dialed Wade's number. Before she could change her mind.

"¡Hola!" his housekeeper answered.

"Tia, this is Jessie Hart. Wade's expecting my call."

"You sure?"

"Positive." Wade had given her the password to get through to him. "I'm calling concerning our tee-off time."

"Oh, sí. Okay, hold on."

Jessie waited until Wade's deep voice sent her pulse skittering. Looking toward the screen, she raised her defenses. "I've got your companion."

"There in the office?"

"No, on my computer screen."

"Oh."

Her hand tightened on the receiver. She could imagine Wade listening, responding, anticipating the results of her search. What did he want? Her? Or her opposite? Had she simply been within arm's reach the other night? No, she couldn't believe that. The passion they'd shared, the heat they'd generated, had been all too real, too consuming, too mind-boggling. Even though two people *wanted* each other didn't mean they *needed* each other.

"When do you want to meet her?" she forced herself to ask.

"As soon as you can set it up."

"Fine." Her nerves felt brittle. It wasn't because of Wade. It wasn't the thought of setting him up with a companion, someone to encourage him during the day, comfort him at night. It was anxiety over her software program and winning her bet with Jack. That's all it was.

Definitely not Wade. Or his need for a damn companion.

Or her desire for him.

# 7

"I APPRECIATE YOUR HELP." Jessie handed the tall, cool blonde a glass of wine. She slid her hip onto the bar stool and watched the door to the restaurant, anxious for Wade to appear.

"Don't even consider it a favor." Heather sipped the wine.

She rotated the glass by the stem and Jessie couldn't help but notice her perfectly manicured nails. They, of course, went with her perfectly coiffed hair. And her perfectly applied makeup. Heather looked the part of a pampered companion. Which made Jessie feel perfectly sick.

Why had the damn computer picked Heather as a match for Wade? There must be a glitch in her program. The tendons at the back of her neck stretched taut. Concern, she thought. No, jealousy. *Nonsense!*

"I consider it a pleasure," Heather said in a silky-smooth Southern accent, the same accent Jessie's mother had pounded out of her as a child. "To be able to help Dr. Wade Brooks with his next book, well, it's an honor."

It was actually the ploy Jessie and Wade had concocted for their agreement. No one would suspect Wade wanted a companion, even if Jessie wished she could use that information to enhance her business prospects. Even if she wanted to call off their agreement and forget matching him up with anyone else. Anyone besides her. Her conflicting emotions made her head pound.

"So..." Heather crossed her legs, rubbing her silk-encased calf against her knee in a provocative move that made the men circling the bar like sharks take notice. "Did I hear you're dating Dr. Brooks?"

"Who, me? Oh, no. Not at all." Jessie felt heat skid along her nerve endings. She could see the woman's interest in the love doctor, calculating her odds, sizing up what chance she might have at knocking Jessie out of contention. How could she answer this delicately? She should imply Heather had a shot when she wanted to say, *He's taken. By me!*

But she wouldn't—couldn't blow this. She had a lot riding on this computer match—her peace of mind and the bet.

The damn bet. Just today Jack had announced a couple he'd introduced were going away for a weekend. Time was running out.

"It's nothing serious." She speared the cherry in her drink with a narrow, red straw. "We've been to dinner a time or two." Okay, tonight would make it twice. If he asked her to stay! "The press blew it way out of proportion."

"Mmm." From Heather's glance, Jessie knew what the woman was thinking—Wade's available. "Sounds promising."

For whom? Jessie fisted her drink and took a sip to steady her nerves. Trouble was, it did the exact opposite, made her daring. A risky state to be in with Wade about to arrive.

"Now..." Jessie took a stern tone, the same one she'd used with subordinates in the corporate world,

"...this evening with Wade is for research. I wouldn't want you to get the wrong idea—"

What was she saying? And why couldn't she stop herself?

But Heather wasn't paying attention. Suddenly her eyes widened. It was as if her whole body went on full man alert, her radar zeroing in on her next prey.

"There he is." Heather swiveled her bar stool, aligning herself with Wade, who had caught sight of Jessie and was heading their way. "Oh, he looks as good as his book jacket. Better. Divine. Delicious."

*Disgusting.* Jessie gulped more of her drink.

Heather patted her arm. "Don't worry about staying. I'm sure you have work to do. I'll be fine with him. Alone."

Jessie's insides lurched with dread, and her smile faltered.

"Wade." Jessie greeted him as he came up the two steps into the bar area. "I'm so glad you were able to join us."

His tanned features looked sharply angled in the shadowy light. He gave her a brief nod, then focused his attention on the honeyed blonde at Jessie's side. When he smiled at Heather, Jessie's temper snapped. But she directed her anger at herself. It was her fault. She could have had him in her bed. But instead she'd practically kicked him out of her house.

"My pleasure." He offered his hand. "I'm Wade Brooks."

"Heather Palmer." She held on to Wade's hand two seconds too long, then slid her fingers along his palm.

Jessie clunked her glass on the wooden counter, sloshing some of its contents over the edge onto her hand. "Uh, Wade—"

"Thank you for volunteering, Miss Palmer."

"Please, call me Heather."

"Heather. A beautiful name." He sent a glance toward Jessie and gave a succinct nod.

What was he saying? That he approved the match? That he wanted her to leave now? Vamoose? Scram? She squeezed the life out of her purse. *I'm not going anywhere.*

Wade moved to Heather's side and leaned one elbow against the bar. "I appreciate you answering some questions for me."

"Oh, whatever I can do to help." Heather gave him a flirtatious wink that had Jessie grinding her teeth.

"Good. Then shall we get a table?" He placed a hand at Heather's back and icy jealousy chilled Jessie's blood.

Stunned, she sat on the bar stool for a hair-splitting second, then launched into action. *I'm not leaving.* It made no sense. It was irrational. But somehow Wade caused her to do the unexpected, the out-of-the-question, the absurd. "I'll be happy to tell the maître d' that we're ready."

"I can handle it." He urged Heather forward and leaned back toward Jessie to whisper, "I can handle everything from here."

"But—"

"I'll call you in the morning for a report."

He was dismissing her. Dismissing her! Jessie wanted to pound him on the back as he turned from her and strode away with the blonde attached like a cufflink to his arm. Actually, she realized, she wanted to crumble into tears.

Well, she wouldn't. She straightened her spine. She wouldn't cry over some man. Not even Wade.

WADE HAD NEVER been so bored in his life. Jessie would not be happy that her computer program had produced such a dull, lifeless match.

He sat across from Heather at their intimate table for two. She ran her bare toe along his shin. He coughed and shifted in his seat. Would the waiter never bring those damn appetizers?

Toying with his knife, twisting it over and over, he contemplated why he'd antagonized Jessie. What the hell had gotten into him? Jessie. She'd gotten under his skin.

He knew his dismissal of her had been his way of trying to prove that the other night had meant nothing to him, as it had clearly meant nothing to her. His pride had been wounded and he'd wanted to prove to her that he was happy with the other fish in the vast singles sea. Or maybe he'd wanted to prove it to himself. Because Jessie was not the type of woman he was looking for.

"I'm sorry for the delay," the waiter said, placing a tray of crab cakes between them.

"I'd like another glass of wine," Heather said.

The waiter nodded and reached for her glass. "And you, sir?"

"Nothing for me." He wanted to remain cold sober. Maybe he could keep himself from driving over to Jessie's. Keep himself from getting in deeper than he already was.

As the waiter disappeared, Wade leveled his gaze on the blonde across from him. She was pretty in a sheltered, plastic surgery way. He'd heard all about her adventurous life following men from city to city, living off her father's trust fund. He'd heard enough. She wasn't his type. She wasn't Jessie.

No! He slammed those thoughts shut. Jessie was completely wrong for him. She was way too much like Tanya. Jessie drove him crazy, consumed his thoughts, filled his dreams, made him feel again.

Angry at himself, he slapped the knife back on the table. "Are you sure you should have another drink? Will you be safe to drive?"

"I didn't bring a car." She gave him a suggestive look. "I guess you'll have to take me home."

Or call a cab, he thought.

WHAT WAS HAPPENING? Not knowing was worse, Jessie decided, than watching some woman fawn all over Wade. Her mind raced with wild scenarios as she paced her office. She imagined Wade sitting in the restaurant, the honeyed blonde draped over his arm like an accessory. Cozy. Intimate. Romantic.

*Nauseating.*

What was wrong with her? Wasn't she supposed to make a successful match for Wade, so she'd win the bet with Jack? So she could get him out of her life? Yes. No. *What the heck is wrong with you, Jess?*

Her jumbled emotions unnerved her. Maybe it was simply anxiety over the computer program. Had it worked? Had it made the perfect match? Would Wade stay the night with the blonde and call Jessie in the morning with a full report?

Her heart contracted. Just what she wanted to hear—how Wade had made love to another woman. When it could have been her! A pang of something—something she'd never felt before—ripped through her.

What was wrong with her? Was she catching a summer flu? Had she gone soft? This was business. Business! *Get over it, Jess. He means nothing to you. Nothing at all.*

The jangle of the phone made her pulse leap and race. She practically jumped over the desk to grab the receiver. Sprawled across its surface, over a stack of questionnaires, she managed a professional tone. "Sole Mates. How may we help you?"

"Jessie? It's Amber." The crackle over the phone revealed her friend was calling on her cell phone.

"Oh, hi." She tried not to sound too disappointed that it wasn't Wade. Her tense body relaxed as she reclined across the top of her desk. "How are you?"

"Exhausted. A long day in court." Jessie could almost hear her friend give a dismissive wave. "How are you?"

"Okay." But she wasn't. She was mixed up, confused. Maybe she could ask Amber for advice. No, her friend wouldn't understand. Their friendship had been forged in setting career goals, hurdling obstacles like men. Amber had always agreed with Jessie's philosophy of keeping focused on work. She would laugh hysterically at Jessie's predicament and then tell her to "Get over it." *Get over him!*

"I saw the publicity photo in the paper. Good going. That ought to bring people in."

"No," Jessie protested, "that wasn't for publicity." She leaned her elbow on the desk, resting the receiver and her cheek into her palm.

"Then it's true? You're dating the famous love doctor?" Amber's voice sounded distant, but distinctly energized.

"Not exactly." But she *wanted* it to be true. Jessie's brow tightened into a frown. She needed to discuss it, analyze it, understand it. But it was all so damn confusing. "It was all a misunderstanding."

"Guess it won't hurt to capitalize on it, though. I was trying to locate Jack. Is he there?"

"Jack?" Never had Amber called for Jack. "How come?"

"Well, um, he called me. I was returning his call."

"Is it business related?" Jessie probed.

"Not exactly."

Stunned, she clutched the phone tighter. "What's going on?"

"Jess, you wouldn't understand. It's, well, kind of crazy. I can't explain it."

*Try!*

"Look I'm about to go under a tunnel. We'll probably get cut off. Will you tell Jack I called?"

"Will do." Confused and hurt by Amber's evasiveness, she leaned farther across her desk to replace the receiver.

"You'll do what?" A sexy male voice shocked Jessie.

With a gasp, she scrambled off the desk and swung around, embarrassed her backside had been pointed toward Wade. Heat stung her. Wade stood in the doorway to her office, humor making his eyes shine like cobalt.

"Working late?" he asked, a slight smile curving his full bottom lip. She remembered too well the feel of his mouth on hers, and her pulse danced.

Her mind raced. What was he doing here? Where was Heather? Hope shot through her. "Is it late? I must have lost track of the time."

*Don't be coy, stupid! Be smart. Grab him. Kiss him!*

But she couldn't. She felt frozen, unable to thaw her emotions to respond.

He sank into one of the leather chairs facing her desk. "You're the consummate business owner, aren't you?"

Defensive, about his charge or because she felt shaky and vulnerable, she leaned back against the edge of her desk and clasped her hands in front of her. "I like what I do. Don't you?"

"Sometimes. I like the research."

Something inside her caught and twisted. "Research like Heather?"

His mouth stretched taut. "I like studying people." He tilted his head to the side, analyzing her as if she were a specimen placed under a microscope. "You're an enigma."

"Me? Why?"

Suddenly he stood and blocked her view of everything, except him. He towered over her. His broad shoulders seemed wider, and she remembered the hard lines and planes of his chiseled muscles. Her throat tightened. She could smell smoke and the faint scent of wine on him. She ached to reach for him, but her arms felt numb.

"Are you drunk?"

"No." He lifted his hand and traced his finger along her jaw. Electricity vibrated through her. "I don't understand how you can forget. How can you shrug off what we shared? How we felt together? How we kissed?"

She couldn't. That was the problem.

She jerked her chin up, breaking contact with him. Still, heat simmered along her nerve endings. All her senses sharpened, became more intense. His gaze felt like a slow, erotic caress. She wanted to touch him, smooth her hands over his broad shoulders, pull him close, taste his kiss once again. This need became a burning hunger inside her, a craving that she knew no one but Wade could fill. Something prevented her from crossing that invisible but palpable line.

"I don't know what you mean. Besides, you certainly seemed to forget all about me when you saw Heather."

"God, you're stubborn." He chuckled. "Do I need to remind you?"

"No." She unclasped her hands and sidestepped away from him, but was still unable to take a complete breath. She prayed he would remind her.

*Grab me. Shake me. Kiss me senseless!*

She realized then that her brain barricaded the needs of her heart. She couldn't quit analyzing, deciphering, trying to understand this wild passion.

His gaze, casual yet sharp, followed her as he sat on the edge of her desk. "Maybe I'm unaccustomed to this dating scene."

"You?" she countered. "The love doctor?"

He released a ragged sigh. "I haven't really dated since Tanya. Occasionally maybe. I went through a stage when I was completely numb. But now I feel..."

Startled by the strain in his voice, she turned to look at him. He raked his fingers through his hair. She remembered the texture of those waves, the thickness, the warmth of his scalp.

"...different. Unsteady. Outmaneuvered."

"Confused?" she asked, knowing exactly how he felt.

"Alive." The blue in his eyes brightened.

"Because of—" Jessie's breath snagged on a jagged shard of jealousy "—Heather?"

He shook his head and took a step toward her. "You."

"Wade." She held up a hand to ward him off. Damn. She didn't need or want this complication. Or did she? "We can't do this." Her pulse leaped erratically. "If Heather wasn't the right one, then I'll have to run the program again."

He clenched his teeth. A tick started in his jaw. "Why are you playing this game?"

"It's not a game." It was real. Her fear, confusion, frustration was too real to imagine or ignore. She had to sort through it all before she made a mistake. "It's not what you or I want. So why start?"

"I don't know."

She understood his confusion, but she couldn't leap forward blindly, the way he seemed ready to do. "Well, I know. I know how it will end." She crossed her arms at her waist to still her trembling limbs and keep from launching herself at him. "So I'm sticking to our agreement.

"Okay," she said, changing the topic, "Heather wasn't right."

"Hell, no." He ground the words out. "And you're not, either. But I can't deny this chemistry, this passion, this craziness between us."

"Then ignore it." Jessie moved around her desk to divert her attention from Wade's heavy gaze. "Don't worry. We can fix the glitch in the program." She settled into her chair, facing the computer. Nervous energy galvanized her. Her fingers flew over the keys as she typed in the different commands. "So tell me, what was wrong with Heather?"

Silence met her answer. She looked over her shoulder. Wade had moved behind her. Startled, she hit the wrong key and the computer squawked.

"Was it the way she looked?"

He shrugged.

Her nerve endings coiled tight. "Was it her sugar-sweet accent?"

His gaze revealed nothing. Okay, he was looking at her. Correction. At her mouth. As if he wanted to kiss her. Her pulse skittered to a halt. If he kissed her, all would be lost. She'd be lost. Until they came up for air. Until reality set in. Then she'd be devastated.

She jerked her attention back to the screen. "Was it her personality? Her hair? The color of her lipstick?"

He moved closer, leaning down, his breath warm on her neck. Desperate to find some way to stop her pulse from galloping and to keep her distance from Wade, she searched for another question, but her mind faltered.

Maneuvering the mouse, she clicked the arrow on Wade's pseudonym.

"You named me Big Foot?" he asked, his voice dipping low into the suggestive range.

*Stupid, Jess, very stupid.*

Ignoring him, she squared her shoulders. "Was Heather too eager? A doormat? Too career-minded?" Her hand tightened on the mouse. Frustration made her turn to look at him once more. "What?"

Humor glinted in the depths of his eyes. "It was her shoes."

THE ANSWER to Jessie's question that night had been easy. Heather wasn't Jessie. Plain and simple. But Wade couldn't tell Jessie that. He could barely accept the truth himself.

And, of course, she was right. They weren't right for each other. Or were they? Maybe he didn't want them to be soul mates. Maybe he was afraid. Hell, yes, he was afraid. Afraid of feeling so deeply again. Afraid of losing again. Afraid of the way Jessie made him feel.

So now he found himself on another covert date, pretending he was on a research mission. The date was fast becoming another nightmare. Quickly. Where did Jessie find these women?

She'd gone to the opposite extreme from Heather. This woman, Jo, liked the natural look. No makeup. No jewelry. No bra. He couldn't say that was a strike against her. She certainly had the body for it. But if that's all he wanted, then he would have taken several fans up on their offers. But it was more than a physical desire. Much more.

"Then I was with a guy named—" Jo snapped her fingers in rapid succession "—Jerry. Yeah, that's his name." She adjusted the strap of her white tank top, which revealed more than it hid.

He made a mental note never to discuss Tanya with a date again. Hearing about other lovers was a definite turnoff.

"Jer was nice, but kind of bookish. He sure knew how to make a gal..." She gulped her margarita and jabbed a chip into the hot sauce. "Well, you know."

He knew, all right. And hearing about her exploits made him uncomfortable, as if he were a voyeur.

"Have you ever done it on a plane?" Jo asked, eyeing him as if he were a tortilla chip to be devoured.

"Excuse me?" Maybe it had been too long since he'd been out with women. But her question shouldn't have surprised him. Not after all the antics women had pulled to meet him over the past year.

"I'm not talking a commercial plane," she said, munching on another chip. "I mean one of those two-seaters." She fanned her face with her hand. "Jerry sure could fly."

Wade made his excuse early, quickly before Jo invited him to take a tour of Dallas in her private plane. At one time in his life an offer such as that would have been too tempting to turn down, but not now. Not when he compared Jo's smile to Jessie's, her shoulder-length bleached hair to Jessie's short-cropped brunette waves, her brown eyes to Jessie's blue-green ones. Each time, Jessie won out. And he knew he should just go on home.

But he didn't. Instead, he drove past Sole Mates. The door and windows were as dark as midnight. He scanned the deserted parking lot but didn't see Jessie's Camry. Disappointment crinkled his disposition.

What was wrong with him? Why did he want Jessie so much? Why did she dominate his thoughts? Permeate his dreams?

Irritated with himself, he headed home. He cranked the sound on his car stereo, turning it to an annoying rock station at an ear-splitting level, and hoped the beat would drive Jessie out of his brain. He rolled down the windows to allow the night air to clear his thoughts. But neither did the trick.

He remembered her clipped tone when she'd called him with the latest computer match. He could see her chin lifted in defiance when he'd wanted desperately to kiss her. He couldn't forget the warmth of her body pressed to him, her breast filling the palm of his hand, her mouth hot and urgent on his. He simply couldn't get her out of his mind.

As he rounded the last corner before his house, he

almost slammed on his brakes. At the end of the block, in front of his two-story, a car crept along the street. The headlights were on low beam, cutting a hazy swath across his sidewalk and lawn. Concern nettled inside him. He reached for his car phone, ready to call the police if this turned out to be a prowler or another crazed fan. Then the car braked and turned into his driveway.

That's when he recognized the make of the car. And the driver. Jessie.

Nudging the accelerator, he advanced down the rest of the street and whipped in behind her, blocking her escape as she'd started to back up and turn around. She braked before she plowed into the front of his car. Stopping the car, he alighted and stalked toward her. His headlights shone like spotlights across his driveway.

"What are you doing?" she asked, irritation sharpening her tone as she met him toe to toe.

"I could ask you the same question." He narrowed his gaze on her. "Spying on me?"

"S-spying!" she sputtered. "Are you insane? I just...well, I thought you might be home and I could, you know, check to see how your date went." She propped her hands on her hips. "So...how'd it go?"

He closed the space between them, braced his hands on the top of her car, trapping her. "Why do you want to know?"

"F-for the program. For my business. Remember? I made you a deal."

"Forget it."

"I don't want to forget it."

"Yes, you do."

"No, I don't. I want to get it right."

"You want to win a damn bet with your brother."

"Yes, but I also want to make my business a success."

He sensed she was as scared as he was, maybe more so. And he wanted to turn the tables on her. "What are you so afraid of, Jessie?"

She jerked her chin. "I am not afraid. Of you. Of anything."

"Uh-huh." He bracketed her waist with his hands, pulled her close, felt her tremble in his arms. His body tightened with need. Desire pumped through his veins. "Prove it."

"The only thing I want to prove is that my computer program works."

"It doesn't."

"Again? It failed again?" Confusion clouded her eyes. "So you didn't like Jo, either?"

"You've got to be kidding."

"You're not helping me redefine the parameters."

"Oh?" He circled her slight body with his arms, refusing to let her escape. "Let me do that for you."

He caught her open mouth and kissed her hard, fast, taking out all his frustrations, releasing his need. But instead of it being depleted, it was rejuvenated. When he felt her soften, her body curve into his, her mouth respond, he severed the kiss. Maybe the way to force her hand was to force her to face her own desire, the passion she wanted to deny.

"What the hell was that?" She looked stunned, shaken.

"Thought that was obvious. Need me to show you again?"

"No."

"You haven't answered a questionnaire, have you?" he asked, keeping her off balance.

"Of course not. I don't—"

He kissed her again. It accomplished two things. One, it shut her up. Two, he needed her as much as he needed air to breathe.

Instantly, her body melted against him. Her arms came around his waist, clinging to him, hugging him tight. Her lips turned to velvet, opening to his probe. His body ignited.

The kiss turned hot, demanding, explosive. Using every ounce of restraint he could muster, he called a halt to it. He'd made his intentions plain. Now it was her move. He wanted her to come to him willingly.

Stepping back, breaking the intimate embrace and the mind-blowing kiss, he took a ragged breath and stared at her. The beams from his car's headlights made her skin look pale, her features stark. He wanted to be gentle, to take her hand tenderly and pull her into his house and make love to her all night. But he knew that wasn't what she needed. Not now. She had to face facts first.

"Prove it to yourself," he said, tossing her a challenge. "Put in your own questionnaire. See if we don't match. Otherwise, you're going to have to admit that Jack's right, that his shoe theory is accurate."

"Never."

He chucked her on the chin affectionately. He would have tried another kiss, but he sensed she would have rebuffed him. "You are so stubborn. Now get out of my driveway and go home. Prove Jack wrong. But you know and I know, we'll be great together. If only you'll give us a chance."

# 8

*TWO STRIKES! One more and you're out of the running, Jess.*

That's what she wanted. Wasn't it?

She could have easily made a colossal mistake. She would have readily followed him into his house and made love to him. Right there. In the marble entryway! With Wade, she seemed to have no willpower, no self-control, no logic.

She knew it was deeper than physical attraction. She cared about Wade, cared too much. He made her feel things she'd never felt before. *Yeah, confused, dizzy, crazed.*

She couldn't—wouldn't get involved with him. What would be the point? A few reckless nights, maybe even months, of mind-altering, heart-changing sex? Eventually he'd want more. After all, he wanted a companion. He didn't want a casual physical relationship. If he did, then he could have chosen any groupie offering him the key to her room.

Not that there was anything casual about the fire that ignited between them each time they touched. If they made love it would consume them, devour her. Body and soul. She'd have nothing left because it would end. A relationship with him had nowhere to go, no place to grow. Her heart would be battered, torn, shredded to pieces.

No. She wouldn't allow that to happen.

So Jessie returned to her office that night with the memory of Wade's kiss urging her away from him. Restless, she intended to run her program again and find another match for him. Winning the bet would ease her suffering. And the sooner she got Wade out of her life, the better.

Settling behind her desk, she stared at a blank questionnaire, toying with an idea, one he'd provoked. Remembering his confession of loneliness, she knew why he'd struck a chord inside her. She was lonely, too. More than she'd ever realized. Maybe she should be searching for a match for her instead of Wade.

Without analyzing anything, she filled out the questionnaire and inserted her answers. She used a code name for herself—Cinderella—and chuckled at the irony. How many times when she was a little girl had her mother read her a different version of that fairy tale? One where she thanked the handsome prince for his offer, then rode in her pumpkin carriage to medical school or Harvard or Wall Street. Her mother would croak if she saw this. This wasn't some fairy tale she was playing. This was dangerous. She remembered how she'd lost her shoe in the steamy dressing room and how he'd returned it, just like Prince Charming.

Backspacing over the code name, she replaced it with Roxy. But that sounded too racy, too sexy, too obvious. Again, she deleted the name and typed in Gertrude. *Better*. Still, her fingers faltered on the keyboard. As she typed in her answers, she questioned her sanity. *What are you doing?* "What are you doing, Jess?"

She blinked at the male voice echoing her own question. Swiveling her chair toward the door to her office, she frowned at her brother. "Jack! What are you doing here so late?"

"I left something in my office. What are you working on?"

"Uh—" She couldn't say she wanted her own date.

"The financials again?" He leaned his shoulder against the doorjamb, his brow folded into a frown. "Everything okay?"

She nodded, feeling as if her brain was mush. "We're much further ahead than I'd anticipated." Easing her hand toward the mouse, she clicked and removed Gertrude's form from the monitor. "I'll be able to cut us both a check at the end of the month. Did you get your messages that I left on your desk?"

"Yeah, thanks."

"The one from Amber?" she prompted.

"Got it."

So he was going to be difficult, eh? "Is something going on between you two?"

"Now you want to play confessional?" He grinned. "When I asked you about the love doctor—"

"Quit calling him that. And Amber's my friend."

He gave a heavy sigh. "Nothing serious. Yet."

"Yet? Are you dating?"

"Seeing each other."

"What's the difference?"

"Commitment."

She slapped her hand against the desk. "I knew it. I predicted it." She tipped her head back and laughed. Throw away her questionnaire and delete Gertrude from the computer! "If things work out for you two then I could win the bet!"

"Nope. You used my theory, not your lame program. I'd win."

She ground her teeth in frustration.

He pushed away from the door. "I better get my stuff and get out of here. You, too."

Distracted by his statement, she gave a slight wave and turned back to her monitor. *Lame program, my foot!*

If Jack could use his dating Amber to win the bet, then two could play that game. A dangerous game.

With a few clicks of the mouse, she pulled up Gertrude again, reversed the program and waited for her match to appear. Anticipation coiled inside her, until she wondered if it might pair her with Wade. What then? Could she ignore that? Was she about to take a giant leap into quicksand?

A faint beep alerted her, drawing her attention to the bottom of the screen. Her pulse faltered. She frowned. Tom Redmond? The sleazy, ambulance-chasing attorney? No way. He wouldn't distract her from Wade, he'd annoy her. She'd met him three days ago when he'd signed up for the executive program. He'd made her skin crawl. A shudder rocked through her. Was she that desperate?

Definitely not. She made a few minor adjustments, including deleting Tom from the computer hard drive. She could always add him later by transferring the backup disk. Then she gave another spin of the proverbial wheel of fate. "Damn."

"What's the matter?" Jack poked his head into her office.

She almost jumped out of her skin. "Haven't you left yet?"

His eyes narrowed, the corners squinting into tiny lines. He shrugged and the golf bag he carried over his shoulder slipped to the floor with a clank and a thud. "Something wrong?"

"It's nothing."

"Doesn't look or sound like nothing." He plopped into the seat opposite her desk, kicked his tennis shoes off and propped his socked feet on her desk. "Come on, sis, fess up."

"Only if you'll kiss and tell."

"We're going swing dancing tomorrow night."

"Oh?" Her voice lilted with an underlying question.

"Don't switch subjects. You haven't been yourself since—"

"I'm fine."

"—since Wade showed up here with your shoe. You know I warned you he could be your prince charming."

Or worst nightmare. "Not likely."

"Wishing?"

She shook her head. But she couldn't force the false denial through her tight throat. That was the problem. She wanted him to be her prince charming. As ridiculous as that sounded. She'd never wanted a prince charming her entire life. Had she lost her mind? Or her heart?

Exhaustion overwhelming her, she leaned back into her chair with a heavy sigh. "I'll tell you what's wrong. It's this program. It's not...well, it's having trouble."

"How are you constructing it?"

"It's not that. It's the questions. I can't get to the heart of what people want. Wade said that would be the problem."

"What, exactly?" Jack asked.

"He said people rarely know what they truly want,

until it's right in front of their face." She'd never wanted a man, her own man, in a permanent way until she'd met Wade. No wonder he scared the starch right out of her.

"That's why my theory works. People buy shoes on impulse. It portrays a life-style. And it reveals so much more."

"Jack." She rolled her eyes.

"I know you like things concrete. You like hard facts and spreadsheets. Well, love, my dear sister, doesn't come on a spreadsheet. There's nothing logical about passion."

"I know that." Or so she was learning.

"Do you?" He rubbed his jaw.

"Jack, you grew up with Father."

"A poor example," he added, "for commitment."

"Exactly. He's always living in the passion-filled moment. One big overgrown hormone."

Jack grinned. "I've been that way for a long time myself. But I'm not our father, Jess. I tried my best to not hurt anyone I dated. You don't have to worry about Amber."

"I know. You'll probably set her up with someone fabulous."

"Not this time." Surprised by his serious tone, she couldn't voice another question. "Did Mother ever discuss their divorce with you?"

"No. But she always told me never to rely on a man."

He nodded. "I don't know what happened, either. But judging from Father's other divorces, I'm sure it was devastating to Mother."

Jessie's back stiffened. She couldn't imagine her mother as one of the simpering saps her father had married in recent years. She'd imagined her mother being too strong-willed, too career-minded for her father's tastes. Their divorce had been final before Jack and she had turned one, so it was all conjecture anyway.

"Mother did fine," she said defensively.

"Yeah, sure. Now almost thirty years after the divorce she's on top of her world. But is she happy? Or is her career a defense mechanism because she was forced into the corporate world by our father?"

"She's happy," Jessie snapped.

"How do you know? She never dates."

"Jack, if Mother wanted a man, then I'm confident she could find herself one. Whatever Mother wants, she gets."

"That's simply my question. Why doesn't she? I think it goes back to the divorce."

"I don't want to discuss this." Jessie looked down at her hands.

"You don't want to look at why you avoid love, either, Jess."

"I do not—" He sent her a quelling look, and she swallowed the denial. "Jack, not everyone's life revolves around the social calendar and whether they have a date Saturday night."

"You still don't get it, do you?"

She fisted her hands. "What?"

"Love. Passion. It's not a game where you chalk up how many dates you've had. Quit being a computerized remake of Mother and live a little."

Her defenses raised like hackles.

"You've been trying your whole life to be like Mother, to be a success, to wear blinders and keep your focus on your damn career. Well, there's more to life, baby sister. All I'm saying is that Mother made her decision, probably because of the pain of divorce. I want you to make your own decisions, not based on Mother or fear."

"I'm not—"

He waved his hand, dismissing her denial before she finished. "Just think about what I said. Don't let this opportunity with Wade pass you by." Grinning to diffuse the tension in the room, he said, "You should go with Amber and me tomorrow night. I'll be demonstrating how my theory works."

She shook her head. "No, thanks. I wouldn't want to be a third wheel on your date."

"It's a research expedition. Amber's not convinced my theory works. Neither are you."

"We're wise beyond our years." Jessie grinned.

"You're the one who pointed out how we both go barefoot. Made me start thinking. Heck, I've used my theory on lots of people but never on myself. How long have I known Amber?"

"Since college. She flew out to see me a couple of times."

"Strange how I never thought of her as my type." He shook his head.

Suddenly she remembered Jack's prediction about her and Wade and felt a shiver shimmy down her spine. Needing to change the subject, she slanted her gaze toward the doorway. "You came back here for your clubs?"

He grinned. "Yeah, I've got a seven o'clock tee-off—" he stood and turned toward the door "—with the love doctor. Want me to put in a good word for you?"

She half rose out of her seat. "Don't you dare."

He gave her a broad wink. "Have a good evening, sis."

Irritation twisting her insides, she tapped her pen against the desk. Jack was wrong. Wade was not the right match for her. Or maybe it was her program. Could pen scratches on paper resemble the fire burning between them? It was chemistry. Sex. Not love ever after. Certainly, it didn't have anything to do with their shoes. She'd prove Jack's theory wrong. And she'd prove she wasn't afraid. Of anything. Including Wade.

Jarring her attention back to the task at hand, she made a few clicks, then arrowed the Start button. She'd forget about ol' Gertrude for the moment. She had more important things to do. Such as getting Wade a companion, so he could get out of her life. The computer hummed as it sought a new match for Big Foot. When it beeped, she jerked her gaze to the bottom of the screen where the potential date was highlighted.

Ginger Cateloni. Ginger? The petite redhead? No way. She was not right for Wade. The woman wore platforms! Powerful emotions resembling anger and jealousy overtook Jessie and she deleted the woman's file.

*What are you doing, Jess?*

*Nothing.*

*Did you really think it would pull up Gertrude's file?*

She pressed her lips together in frustration. *Maybe. No. Okay, yes. Yes, dammit!*

Then she ran the program again.

This time another name popped onto the screen. Madeleine Thompson. Who was she? Jessie didn't care. She deleted her, too.

She kept right on deleting women as if she were on a revenge-seeking mission. They weren't right for Wade. She knew it. She deleted until there was only one female left in the computer bank. Gertrude.

Going out with Wade would simply prove that Jack's theory didn't work.

*Sure, Jess, believe whatever you want.*

GOLF SHOES did not personify the man of her dreams. Jessie smiled with self-satisfaction as she watched Jack and Wade walk across the green toward the last hole, the tassels and leather fringe on the tops of their golf shoes flapping with each step. But her gaze didn't stop there. She noticed the crease in his khakis and followed the line up to the pleats along his narrow waist. She remembered dark hair arrowing down to—

*Jess! Whatever this is, you've got it bad!*

After Jack dunked his ball, Wade clapped him on the back. Together they headed toward their carts and drove along the short, winding road toward the clubhouse, where she was waiting.

Jack saw her first and waved. Then Wade gave a nod of recognition. She could almost see his muscles tense as hers coiled with anticipation. She couldn't wait to tell him about his next date.

"Who won?" she asked as they approached.

"You're not supposed to ask that," Jack said, his smile slicing into a thin line.

"Then congrats, Wade."

He grinned, obviously pleased with his success this morning.

"I've got a meeting in half an hour," Jack said, "so I'll shower and run."

"Be careful," Wade said as Jack headed toward the door.

Her brother paused midstride and arched an eyebrow. "What do you mean?"

"Some lady has been cornering men in the shower."

"Hadn't heard that." Jack gave a slow, eager grin. "But I'll be ready for her." With a wave, he disappeared into the clubhouse.

Jessie felt her cheeks flame. "You're never going to let me live that down, are you?"

"Not anytime soon." He leaned his hip against the porch rail. "So, what are you doing here?"

She twisted her purse straps around her fingers. Her nerves jangled together. "I have news for you."

"Oh?"

"I've found you another match."

"Already?" His brow creased into a noticeable frown. "Let's forget this whole thing. After all—"

"No, no. This one will be different." Panic pumped through her veins. "You'll see. You have to meet her."

"Hmm. I don't know. The last two attempts weren't very successful. And you know what I want."

"I know." She felt breathless. She sensed too much was at stake. The bet. Her heart. "I think I've found the problem—er, solution in the program."

He slanted his gaze at her. "This is the last one. I'm not cut out for this. Set it up. I'll be there."

"Good." How surprised Wade would be to find she was his date. He didn't need to know it was to prove Jack wrong. "The lady already agreed to meet." She held her breath. "Tonight."

His frown deepened. "I can't."

"What? But..." Her heart jackhammered. Did he

have a date of his own? One he'd set up? With one of his groupies?

"It's for business. Jack's going to show me how his shoe theory works. I might incorporate it into my next book."

"You're going swing dancing with Jack and Amber?"

"Yeah."

Her mind spun out of control. Was this Jack's way of dumping her friend, setting Amber up with Wade? Maybe he thought they wore compatible shoes, too. Oh, damn. Why hadn't she taken Jack's offer to go with them? Damn. Damn. Damn.

Wade's gaze narrowed on her. "Why don't you come along?"

"Well, I..." She paused. Wasn't that what she wanted? To spend more time with Wade? There was plenty of time for her to be his official date. "Sure. I'll be there. Might be fun to see Jack's theory in action."

And secretly test it at the same time.

WADE SAT NEXT TO JESSIE at the bar. The big band music with a decided rock beat blared in the background. Instead of wingtips, saddle shoes and Jack's theory on his mind, all Wade could think about was slow, deep kisses...desperate, hungry kisses, and kisses that could ignite the soul.

Jessie's kisses.

He tilted his beer bottle to his lips and tried to keep his attention off her. He watched the dancers gyrating, hopping and swinging to the rhythm. Amber and Jack had already kicked off their shoes and were kicking up their heels on the dance floor. The evening felt as if he'd stepped back in time to the days of Glenn Miller music and Rita Hayworth pinups. The toe-tapping music seemed to put a spring in everyone's step and a smile on their faces. Even Jessie was moving her foot in rhythm with the band, and the movement drew Wade's gaze like a magnet.

She leaned against his shoulder. "What makes this shoe theory work?"

"Universal truths, like horoscopes and psychological classifications."

She laughed. "Like Scorpio represents passion."

"So do stilettos." His gaze slipped for a moment to her shapely leg and the pump dangling from her toe. She might not be wearing stilettos, but he'd definitely seen passion in her blue-green eyes. He met her gaze again and a shimmer of electricity skittered between them.

She cleared her throat and inched away from him, once again denying and rejecting what could be between them. Frustration knotted his stomach.

"Maybe." She took a sip of wine. "Want to know about your date I've set up for tomorrow?"

He wanted to focus on here and now. On Jessie. Her zeal for wanting to set him up with a companion was admirable, but damn irritating. "Not really."

"No?" She looked surprised. "Why?"

"I'd like to get to know the lady myself. Don't want to get my hopes up or reject her before we've met. Wouldn't be fair—to her, to me, or your program."

"Oh." She rolled the bottom edge of her wineglass along the paper napkin.

"Okay. If you insist." He took a pull on his bottle of beer and braced himself. He could withstand listening about his next blind date, as long as it kept Jessie talking. He loved seeing her eyes sparkle with passion—

which seemed to be only when she spoke of work. Or after one of their kisses. "What's her name?"

"Name?" Startled, she stared at him, then plucked at the corner of her napkin, tearing the paper.

"She does have a name, doesn't she?"

"Uh, yeah, of course. It's, uh, Gertrude."

"Gertrude?" He couldn't help but envision a gray-haired woman wearing a bun and half glasses. "Hmm. Sounds different." Boring. "What's she like?"

Jessie shrugged. "I'll let you tell me." She shifted on the bar stool, tugging her skirt along her thigh. "Let's try Jack's theory out before he gets back. Pick a shoe and we'll figure out who the person should dance with."

"Okay." He appreciated the divergence in the conversation. He didn't want to think about going out with someone other than Jessie, especially someone by the name of Gertrude. But it didn't matter what her name was. She wouldn't be Jessie.

"See that guy." She indicated a man a few seats away who wore scuffed loafers. "He's going to hit on that lady."

"The one in that skimpy red dress?"

"Look at the shoes, Wade. The shoes."

He grinned. "Oh, yeah." He slanted his gaze down the woman's stockinged legs to her feet stuffed into five-inch heels. Sexy shoes. Strange how they didn't affect him the way Jessie's did. "Hope she's got an appointment with a podiatrist tomorrow. You think she can dance in those?"

"She didn't come here to dance. And that's certainly not what he wants."

"Sure he does. He wants to do the horizontal..."

Jessie elbowed him. "Question is, will he score?"

Wade looked from the loafers to the stilettos. He shook his head. "Won't work."

"Why?" Jessie challenged. She always challenged him. And somehow he liked it. Liked her. Way too much.

"He wants her too much." The way he wanted Jessie too much. It was dangerous, foolish, pointless. But he couldn't help himself. He should take his own advice—be more aloof. He'd laid his cards on the table with Jessie too soon and frightened her off. "And the lady likes the chase."

"You're making this up. What does that have to do with shoes? How can you tell?"

He shrugged. "Maybe it's the look in his eye."

"You're supposed to be focusing on his shoes," Jessie reminded him. "Besides, she doesn't look like she could chase after anyone in those shoes."

"Ah, but she doesn't have to. She likes to be chased. But she's very selective about who catches her."

Ignoring the couple they had been dissecting, he studied Jessie, the wispy bangs that curled over her forehead, the way her hair looped behind the delicate shell of her ear, her long, sloping neck. He was so close that he could have placed a playful kiss against her warm skin. But he restrained himself. He had to wait. He had to let Jessie make the next move, when she was ready. *If* she'd ever be ready.

He took another swig of his beer. "Sorry. Can't help forgetting about the shoes. I'm a psychologist. I study the entire person. Not one compartment."

He swept his gaze over Jessie, along her slim curves covered by the pale blue sheath dress. Heat compressed his abdomen, burned a hole through his defenses. He wanted her. But what would he do with her once he got her?

"Here he goes." She grabbed his arm, focusing his attention on the man moving toward the red-dressed woman. "Ooh, shot down midsentence. Ouch."

Wade nodded and wondered if he kissed Jessie right here at the bar if she'd shoot him down, too.

No. He wouldn't make that mistake again. It was up to her now. She had to want him as much as he wanted her. No regrets. No turning back.

"So," she said, "you were right." Her blue-green eyes filled with admiration. "I'm impressed."

"About what?" Jack led a breathless Amber by the hand.

"My God," she said, collapsing onto a stool, huffing and puffing as if she'd just run a marathon, "that's hard work. What happened to the good ol' days when we did the hustle?"

"I never did the hustle," Jack said.

"Missed the polyester disco phase myself." Wade ordered Jack a beer and Amber a glass of water.

"At least it's not as embarrassing as line dancing," Jack commented.

Wade rolled his eyes and groaned. Some long-ago date had dragged him into a country and western dance hall to learn line dancing and he'd wanted to crawl right out the back door.

"Well, learning to do the swing couldn't be as difficult as figuring out Jack's shoe theory," Jessie announced.

"It's simple," Wade said.

"See, it's not so hard." Jack took a long pull on his beer.

"It was dumb luck," Jessie countered. "He guessed. But he can't explain why it worked."

"Sometimes it's simply instinct, Jess," Jack proclaimed. The two men clicked beer bottles in a silent salute.

Jessie frowned and sipped her wine. Amber gulped her water.

"Here," Jack offered, "I'll give you a demonstration.

"See that cowboy standing like a fish out of water?" When they nodded and focused on the lanky man wearing a Stetson, Jack continued. "He's got his boots polished, his belt buckle shining, and he's going to offer to buy a drink for that woman over there, the one with the two-toned strapped pumps."

"You mean, the blonde with the Texas-size hair?" Wade asked.

"Yeah. And the silicone—"

Amber punched Jack in the shoulder. "You're supposed to be looking at the shoes."

Wade chuckled. "Reminds me of your receptionist. What's her name?"

"Brandy," Jessie answered. "But she's gone."

"Gone?" Amber glanced toward Jack.

"Long gone. Like to the Bahamas on her honeymoon." Jack grasped Amber's hand.

"What happened?" Wade asked. "Did she find herself an oil tycoon with deeper pockets?"

"Nope. A cowboy."

Wade blinked. Amber kissed Jack. Jessie laughed.

"You didn't set this one up with a pal?" Amber asked.

"She didn't give me much time."

He nodded toward the nearby woman with the big

hair and bigger breasts. "But what about them? What do you think is going to happen over there? Will he get to buy her a drink?"

"Means nothing except she's thirsty," Jessie protested.

"From the looks of those diamond studs in her ears, she could buy her own winery," Wade said jumping into the discussion. "But if she lets him buy her a drink it means she's open. She might reject him later but it means her first impression of him was positive."

"Maybe she's desperate or lonely or stupid," Amber added.

Jessie laughed. "It won't work. She's decked out in forties attire, all primed for this atmosphere, and he's in cowboy boots. She'll rebuff him. He's not her type. No way."

"I agree," Amber said, sucking on a piece of ice.

"Wrong," Wade disagreed, throwing in his two cents.

"Why?" Jack asked.

Crossing his arms over his chest, he studied the couple, the woman's flirtatious toss of her head, the man hooking his thumb in his belt loop. "Maybe she's adventurous. She's bored with the average Joe, the yuppie business suits."

Jack shook his head. "Nah. It's money. And she recognizes it like a long-lost cousin. He's wearing primo custom boots. His grooming might say country, but it's impeccable, even down to a manicure. Money always attracts money."

A second later the lanky cowboy signaled a waiter to bring the lady the drink of her choice.

"That's cheating," Jessie protested, "you're only supposed to look at their shoes."

"The shoes represent personal preferences," Jack explained. "Comfort. Exquisite taste. Laziness. Work-aholic. Pampered. High maintenance. Low mainte-nance. And everything in between."

"Why can't that be input into a computer pro-gram?" Jessie slid her fingers through her short locks with exasperation.

"Some of it is very subjective," Wade added. "It re-quires keen observational skills. And honesty. Not ev-erybody is so truthful with themselves. Certainly not when filling out a questionnaire to find themselves a date or a lifelong partner. It's the same ascribed theory as folks putting on their best facade when going on a date. Takes a while for the facade to fade into the real person. Sometimes years."

Jessie's brow compressed into a frown.

"Don't overanalyze it," Amber suggested. "Go dance. Come on, Jack." She pulled him toward the dance floor.

Jessie stared at Wade. He stared back. Should he jump at the chance? Or remain aloof and wait for her to crawl back?

"Do you know how to swing?" She waved her hand toward the dancers.

"Not at all."

"Me, neither." Her mouth pulled to one side.

"But..." he offered, trying to read her expression.

"Yeah?" She looked eager, her eyes shining. And he took that as an invitation.

"I'm willing to give it a shot, if you've got insur-ance."

She leaned back against the bar. "Insurance?"

"On your toes. In case I stomp on them."

She grinned and reached for his hand. A spark shot

along his nerve endings at her warm touch. "Come on, then. Let's give it a try. We'll hobble out of here together."

He clasped her hand, entwining his fingers with hers, and led her through the thickening crowd, weaving through the maze of tables toward the wooden dance floor. Their first steps were hesitant as they paid more attention to the dancers surrounding them than to each other. Wade tried to avoid bumping into strangers. But as he got the basic steps down, pulling Jessie toward him, turning her out and pulling her back to him like a yo-yo, his attention focused on her, her supple, graceful movements, her warm, vibrant smile. And for the first time in years, his heart felt light and carefree.

Breathless, Jessie leaned into him. Her hand covered his thudding heart. "You've taken lessons, haven't you?"

"Not one."

She gazed up at him, her face flushed, her eyes bright, her lips parted. It took every ounce of restraint to not dip his head and kiss her. "Then how did you catch on so fast?"

"I'm an observer by nature." He shrugged, pleased he'd somehow impressed her. "And it's not much different than the polka or the Texas two-step. I simply added more of a bounce."

"You two-step?"

"Sure, doesn't everyone who lives in Dallas?"

She shook her head. "You'll have to teach me."

"My pleasure." He pulled her closer, then felt a hard clap on his shoulder. Turning, he scowled at Jack.

"Not bad, you guys."

Amber joined them in the center of the dance floor. "Y'all sure do make a cute couple."

Wade's gaze collided with Jessie's. He knew that statement could scare her off permanently. Strange how it didn't make him want to run anymore. He hoped he hadn't lost her for good now.

# 9

"ARE YOU SURE about this, Jess?" she asked herself, her voice echoing in the stillness of her house.

No, she wasn't sure. Heck, she wasn't sure about anything anymore. Especially about Wade. In fact, where he was concerned, she just might have lost her mind. And her heart.

This night could either prove her program and help her win the bet, or it could be her undoing. She couldn't contemplate that now. She had ten minutes to get to the designated rendezvous spot for their surprise date.

She stared at herself in the mirror for another second, snapped on her other sterling-silver earring and checked her lipstick one last time. "Okay," she whispered to herself, "there's no turning back now."

*I'm not turning back. I'll face this. Without fear.*

*I want Wade, dammit. I need him. What's wrong with that?*

That subtle but distinct change in her feelings surprised her. She'd desired her share of men in the past, and she certainly couldn't deny that she desired Wade now, but she'd never *needed* a man.

Hadn't her mother taught her she could stand on her own two feet? That a woman could be strong, powerful, resilient without a man by her side? Her sudden weakness over Wade unnerved her.

She didn't have time to process the new, uneasy feelings. Either she needed to act on them or leave Wade waiting. She'd given him the time and place to meet Gertrude. She could picture him standing beneath the shade of an oak tree, checking his watch, running his fingers through his hair, perplexed as to why his date was late. The choice between standing him up and seeing him tonight was a no-brainer.

"Here goes nothing," she whispered, silently praying he wouldn't laugh when she arrived instead of "Gertrude."

With a shaky breath, she slipped on her slinky black sandals and left her house. She pressed her hand against her fluttering heart. Her skin tingled where she'd sprayed perfume on her pulse points. A balmy, summer breeze ruffled her hair.

Sliding behind the wheel of her Camry, she readjusted the skirt of her sundress. Maybe it wasn't a practical choice for a picnic. But she wasn't in a practical mood. If she was going to face passion straight-on, then she had to be ready.

But it was seeing Wade sitting on a wooden bench a few minutes later as she cruised past the park that made her feel vulnerable, shaky and light-headed.

*You're being ridiculous, Jess. You're simply hungry.*

Yeah, hungry for Wade.

WADE CHECKED HIS WATCH for the twelfth time. Had he misread Jessie's directions? Maybe Gertrude had changed her mind.

Antsy to get this date over with, he tapped his loafer against the thick carpet of grass. He felt as if his starched shirt and khakis were wilting beneath the oppressive heat. Sweat beaded his forehead. His gaze followed the descent of the orange sun dipping below the horizon. The park lights flickered then surged as they came on full force.

The branches of a nearby bush rustled and he peered at it closely, wondering if Jessie might not be lurking, watching, spying on him. A squirrel scampered out from under the limbs and pounced on an acorn.

*You're losing it, Brooks.* Why would he think Jessie was watching him? Then again, she had tracked him down in the locker room. She had driven by his house, checking to see if he'd taken his date home that night. What would she do next? And why would she set up a date here, in a park of all places? It all seemed strange to him. She certainly kept him off balance.

What seemed even more odd was a woman agreeing to meet a stranger in a deserted park. What was wrong with an air-conditioned restaurant? Did Gertrude have some weird phobia and need therapy more than a date?

His nerves twisted tight with wariness. He'd met enough loony-tune women over the past year to question the motives of most. Of course, he reasoned, Gertrude would have already heard of him. He was, after all, the renowned Dr. Brooks. Who would be afraid of him? Or, he shrugged, maybe the lady already knew him. Why did that make him jittery?

He remembered Jessie laughing about the ludicrous dates she'd sicced on Jack. *Great.* Maybe he should keep an eye out for a too friendly poodle....

Rolling his shoulders back, he stretched out his arms, flexed his hands, cracked his knuckles. "Okay," he whispered, "let's get this over with once and for all."

Then he'd go home and forget wanting or needing a companion. It had been a foolish decision. He realized now it might simply have been a rationalization to see Jessie again. And that was a lost cause. She'd made her feelings abundantly clear about not getting involved with him. He wasn't about to get a concussion, banging his head against a closed door.

The soft footfall of someone walking behind him alerted him. He turned abruptly, craning his neck, squinting against the waning light to see who it could be. An elderly gentleman strolled past, leading a tiny white poodle by a leash. Wade didn't know if he felt relief or increased tension.

The poodle's owner gave a brisk nod, and Wade managed a polite but wary, "Good evening."

When he turned back around, he felt his heart slam to a halt. He blinked once, twice, unable to believe what he saw.

Like a vision, Jessie stood several feet in front of him, wearing a black dress. The thin straps revealed her tanned shoulders, the bodice tapered down to a point between her breasts, and the short flaring skirt showed off her long, shapely legs. She wore a pair of feminine sandals, the little straps criss-crossing over the top of her foot. Okay, he could now add mirages to his latest list of daydreams and fantasies. What had gotten into him?

"Good evening," she said, her voice as soft as the subtle breeze stirring the warm summer air, and as unsure as he felt. He knew then he wasn't imagining things.

"W-what are you doing here?" He looked behind her for a woman who might match the name of his date. The sidewalk was deserted. "Where's Gertrude?"

"I'm Gertrude." She gave a slight lift to her shoulder. "If you'd rather it was someone else, then I'll go."

"Wait!" he called out as she started to turn. "I don't understand."

An embarrassed smile pulled at the corners of her mouth enticingly. "I did as you suggested. I put my own questionnaire into the computer bank and gave it a whirl. And guess what?"

Understanding she'd reached her own threshold and was ready to give a relationship with him a chance, he felt anticipation coil inside him. "It gave you a new name?"

She gave a breathy laugh. "It matched me with you—Big Foot."

He stood, his legs unsteady, his pulse racing. He wasn't sure what he was getting into, but he couldn't back away now. He felt the magnetic pull toward her as surely as he remembered her kiss.

"I—is that all right?" She clasped her hands at her waist, twisting her fingers in doubt. "If not, then I can find you someone else. I mean—"

He stepped forward, closing the gap between them, cutting her off midsentence as he swooped down to steal a kiss. A kiss he'd been dreaming about for days. Her lips were supple, soft as dew, sweet as honey. It took every ounce of discipline to release her. For now.

Grazing her jawline with his thumb, he said, "I'd take you over Gertrude anyday."

She gave a shaky smile and released a pent-up breath. He felt nervous energy ripple between them.

"Why a park, though?" he asked.

She glanced around the wooded area and up at the

darkening sky where the stars winked palely like tiny diamonds. As the sky turned as black as Jessie's dress, the stars took on a new brilliance.

"You'd already bought me a nice dinner." She met his gaze squarely. "Remember?"

How could he forget that night? Or the kiss they'd shared in front of photographers? Or those in her living room or the few in front of his house?

"So," she continued, "this was my treat. I thought I'd make you dinner. A picnic dinner."

"You made dinner?" he asked, incredulous.

"Well, okay, I had it catered. But I chose everything on our menu, including the wine. I hope you like it."

ACTUALLY, she wouldn't have minded if they'd skipped dinner altogether. Then again, her nerves knocked crazily together and she suddenly felt like a teen on her first car date.

They found a secluded spot, away from the playground of swings and teeter-totters. It was sheltered by live oaks and honeysuckle bushes. Fresh-cut grass and daisies perfumed the air. Wade carried the basket of food she'd left in her trunk and Jessie spread a red-checked blanket on the ground. She leaned back against a tree trunk and Wade settled next to her.

She could smell the faint scent of cologne on his warm skin. She wanted to touch him, to kiss him as he'd kissed her earlier, but for some reason she held back, nervous, uncertain. It wasn't like her at all.

The park lights blazed from a distance, sending pale vestiges of light to their secluded spot. Through the branches above them, she could see the stars twinkle and the soft moon glow like a luminous opal. As Wade opened the bottle of wine, Jessie sighed. This was exactly how she'd imagined the evening unfolding. *Better.*

Before, when she'd put such high hopes on a romantic evening with other men, either they suddenly weren't as attractive as they'd once been or they'd come on too strong, too domineering. But not Wade. He seemed content to watch her or trace the back of her hand. His virile gentleness overwhelmed her, endeared her to him more and more. He treated her with respect, not as a prized possession.

Pouring the Chardonnay, he clinked his glass against hers. Worried he might make a toast that was too intimate, too powerful, too possessive, she felt her chest tighten and she said, "To tonight."

"Definitely," he added. His gaze felt like a bold caress, and she trembled. "A night I'll treasure."

"Salmon," she said, grabbing the first coherent thought in her head. "I brought salmon. I hope you like it."

He gave an amused smile, the corners of his eyes crinkling as he watched her fumble in the basket for the cold, sliced salmon. She pulled out plates and napkins, along with an array of containers with fruits and vegetables, breads and cheeses. Her pulse throbbed. Her hands fluttered like a nervous butterfly unable to land. Keeping herself busy, her gaze off Wade, helped settle her feelings into place.

Leaning back on an elbow, he raised a bunch of grapes and nipped at the ripened fruit with his lips, plucking off pieces of fruit then chewing them thoughtfully. "This is the life."

"All you need now is a harem," she said, fanning him with a napkin.

He focused on her again, his eyes dark as midnight,

but illuminated with desire, as the moon illuminates the night sky. "All I need is you." As quickly as he'd captured her with his gaze, he released her and bit off another grape. "But then, I've been telling you that for some time."

"Yes, you have." She smoothed her skirt over her legs, crossing them demurely at her ankles. What was wrong with her? Why did Wade make her so nervous? He was just a man. It wasn't as if she were a virgin!

He rolled onto his side. "You told me more than once that you didn't want me." He chuckled. "You made that very clear in the locker room."

Blushing, she remembered yanking off his towel and giving him a disinterested once-over. It had been the best acting job of her life. She should have won an Oscar for her performance.

His smile faded as he rubbed his jaw. "And you didn't beat around the bush in my driveway the other night. So what changed your mind?"

She spread a pink salmon slice across a rye cracker. Her insides felt jittery and flaky. "I don't know. I haven't analyzed my feelings."

"I thought you analyzed everything."

"I did. I do. I mean, I don't know what I mean anymore. I couldn't come up with a good enough reason not to come. I guess I rose to your challenge."

He covered her hand for a brief, tantalizing second. She chewed the salty fish.

"I admire that in you."

"You do?"

"I don't think it's the first time you've acted on instinct or the first time you've accepted a challenge. You're not one to back away from anything."

*See! I'm not afraid. I can handle this...this crazy passion with Wade.*

He popped another grape into his mouth. "I've always been contemplative, overanalytical. Least, that's what—"

Perplexed that he'd cut himself off, she tilted her head to the side. "What?"

He closed off his emotions as quick as a shutter. "So how did you come up with the name Gertrude?"

She laughed at his question and obvious change of subject but accepted it willingly before things took a serious turn. "I have to admit, I reveled in your expression the other night when I told you her name."

After preparing him a salmon cracker, she held it out to him. When he opened his mouth, she hesitated only a second, then slid the cracker onto his tongue. His lips grazed her fingers and anticipation shimmied down her spine.

Covering her surprise at how he so easily affected her, she said, "Actually, I needed a code name. I couldn't put my name in the computer banks."

"Why not?"

"Because, I'm one of the owners."

"So?"

"So," she said, her mind racing, her pulse thrumming, "it's not right. I'm not looking—"

"But you are looking for someone, Jessie," he said, his voice deep, resonant. "Or you wouldn't be here with me."

"I'm here because I want to be. But that doesn't mean I'm looking for anything perm—"

He pressed his fingers to her lips, sending sparks down her spine. "Let's not analyze this tonight. Let's just enjoy it...each other. All right?"

She nodded. Her throat compressed. Her lips yearned for more than the touch of his fingertips.

Rolling onto his back, Wade placed his hands beneath his head and stared up at the constellations. "Jack told me he would have matched us together."

"His shoe theory is—"

"It has merits. More humor than substance. But I can see how it works. Your brother's a born psychologist, but it's intuitive for him. As natural as breathing. As instinctive as denying and hiding your feelings."

"Me?"

He gave her a perceptive look.

"Okay, maybe that's true. Could I claim that I'm not in touch with my feminine side?"

"Not dressed like that." He gave her a curl-your-toes smile.

She blushed from the inside out. Watching his chest rise and fall with each steady breath, she wondered why she felt an invisible band tightening around her chest, restricting her breathing. Was it those emotions he'd spoken of rising to the surface? Or simple desire?

There was nothing simple or uncomplicated about her feelings for Wade. They seemed to be growing, changing, evolving in ways that surprised, exasperated, and overwhelmed her.

She noticed a few silver strands woven through his dark hair, and she couldn't keep herself from running her fingertips through the thick waves. He continued talking in slow, rhythmic tones that soothed and melted her insides. But she wasn't listening to what he was saying. She couldn't concentrate on anything but the physical fascination, his warmth, the tickling sensation of his hair against her palm, the need to be held by him.

While she fed him Brie and strawberries, she listened as he talked about getting his undergraduate degree. "That's the trouble with psych majors. I diagnosed myself, my friends, family, professors as being psychotic, schizophrenic or obsessive compulsive. Of course, in some cases those might have applied."

She smiled softly. "Why did you go into psychology?"

"I sort of fell into it. I was originally a finance major. I took Psych 101 as an elective. To be near a girl."

A strange sensation pulled at her. Instinct told her the answer before she asked the question. "Your wife?"

He nodded but seemed reluctant to have admitted as much. "We weren't married then. She thought it would be a good class for her, since she was getting a journalism degree. I thought it'd be fun. But I really took to it. It was fascinating learning about people, why they acted the way they did.

"Tanya wanted to bring injustices in the world to light. And I developed a burning desire to help others gain control of themselves and their lives."

"But you're not in practice now? You don't see patients, do you?"

"I do volunteer work at a free clinic, but that's all."

"Why?"

He pushed up to his elbows. "I realized I didn't know enough."

"You knew enough to write your book."

"That was based on my dissertation and personal experience." He shrugged. "That was more a cleansing for me. I didn't write it for money. I didn't tell people how to find their soul mates, just that they existed and how to recognize the one. I suppose it did help people. Or at least gave them hope." He looked at her then. "Sole Mates will help people, too."

"You think?"

"Definitely."

She frowned. "But it hasn't helped you."

"Sure it has." His hand closed on her ankle. "It brought me you."

Her heart faltered. "W-what I meant was..."

"You didn't really think you were benefitting society, did you?"

"No, not really. I'm a computer programmer. That's not typically seen as a social service."

"Maybe you're not curing AIDS or cancer, but that's exactly what you're providing—a social service."

She gave him a broad smile. "Would you like some dessert?"

He gave her a look that could have melted an ice cream factory. Tracing his finger along the curve of her calf, he stirred heat deep in her belly. "What did you have in mind?"

"Chocolate?" Her voice actually squeaked and she could have died of embarrassment.

He gave a slight shake of his head and traced the line of her ankle.

"P-pecan pie?" She tried to contain the shiver he aroused.

"Are those my only choices?" His voice was deep and rich as the flourless chocolate cake she'd sampled that afternoon.

Without waiting for her to answer, he loosened the strap on her sandal and slipped it off her bare foot. "I do like these shoes. Not as businesslike as your others."

"I wasn't coming here on business."

"Good." His hands were warm and enveloping as they folded around her heel and ankle. With infinite tenderness and erotic assuredness, he smoothed his hands down her foot and began massaging the ball of her foot with his thumbs in slow, deepening circles.

Closing her eyes, she sighed with pleasure. A fluttering developed deep in her abdomen and spread to her limbs. "This is better than chocolate. More addictive."

He chuckled. "Less calories, too."

"We could start a whole new trend in cookbooks."

Pressing along her arch, making her tremble, he said, "I can see us on Jerry Springer's show. 'How to make your wife, girlfriend or lover sizzle.' Might offer you a new form of publicity for Sole Mates."

She laughed. "I don't think that's the clientele we're aiming for."

"That's a relief."

He dipped his head and placed a kiss on the bottom of her foot. Her breath caught in her throat. She felt the warm, moist point of his tongue as he tickled her arch. A shudder rocked through her.

"Uh, Wade," she said, her voice breathy, her heart trembling, her body yielding to what she knew would happen. She gave in to the sensations and feelings willingly. With her eyes wide-open, her mind shut to its many questions. Her heart remained wary but hopeful. Beneath heavy lids, she gazed at Wade. "Maybe we should have dessert at my place."

# 10

CHOCOLATE, roses and candlelight romance could be incorporated later. As well as sexy lingerie, hot tubs and champagne. Right now, Wade had no desire for sugary desserts or potent port, distractions or more delays. He only had a raw, dangerous hunger for Jessie.

As she tossed the keys onto the entryway floor, she slapped her hand against the light switch. He blinked, his eyes accustomed to the darkness outside. She gave him a suggestive smile that turned his blood to liquid heat. Automatically, he reached for her, fitting her body against his, aligning their chests and hips. He felt her breasts press against him, and desire pulled like a taut rope in his gut.

He cupped her jaw. "I've been waiting it seems like a lifetime for this."

Hooking her hands behind his back, she gazed up at him. Heat swirled in the blue-green depths of her eyes like a whirlpool tugging at him, pulling him down into the frenzied, riotous, wild dark world of desire. "Was I wearing out your patience by making you wait?"

He kissed her lightly, nipping playfully at her full bottom lip. He tasted the sweet stickiness of strawberries. "I would have waited a lot longer for you."

And he would have, he realized, which unraveled

the edges of his confidence. What had she done to him?

Tilting her head, she slanted her mouth across his and whispered, "Welcome to my house."

And your life. For he knew he didn't just want one night with Jessie. He wanted more. Much more.

He breathed in her elusive scent, swallowed her candied taste and relished the feel of her body nestled so close to his. She was thin but not too thin, with enough padding to make things interesting. He couldn't wait to explore each nuance, every flat plane and tempting curve. He smoothed the palms of his hands down her back, along the dip at the base of her spine, then up along her sides until he felt her tremble. His thumbs brushed the fullness of her breasts, and need coiled within him.

"Follow me," she said, her voice husky, her hand grasping his and leading him into what he assumed was her living room. The light from the entryway cast shadows around the room like clothes tossed carelessly around a rumpled bed. She kissed him soundly, as if pulling the very breath out of him, but infusing him at the same time with heart-pumping life.

Walking backward, keeping her gaze locked on his, she began unbuttoning his shirt, slipping her hands inside to run them over his contracting muscles. They left his shirt flung over the sofa and continued moving down a narrow hallway.

He felt his heart pummeling his rib cage. It had been a long time since he'd been with a woman. And even longer since it had meant something deep and personal. "I take it you know where we're going."

In answer, she slipped her hand around his waist,

then down his back to cup his buttocks. "Trust me on this one."

"Implicitly."

She turned away from him, and he followed, as if an invisible magnet drew him to her. In the middle of the hallway, he caught her, hooked an arm around her middle and successfully slid her zipper down her dress. He traced the length of her back with his hand. She was warm, so hot, like liquid velvet.

Squirming, she wiggled free of his hold. She cast a flirtatious look over her shoulder then shrugged out of her skimpy dress, revealing black lace panties that hugged her narrow hips and cupped her shapely backside. His gaze followed the curve of her back up to her shoulders. She wore nothing on top, no slip, no bra. One less barrier between them. His throat went dry, and his pulse pumped hot and fierce.

At the end of the hall, she turned, hugging the door frame to what he assumed was her bedroom. Her arm covered her breasts. She slid one leg up along the molding in a slow, leisurely fashion, pointing her toe, making his trousers too tight and his control slip another notch. Slowly she slipped off one sandal at a time. Then crooking her finger, she whispered, "This way."

He didn't need neon lights to show him which way to go. As he reached her, she started to scamper away again, teasing him. He sensed her nervousness as surely as he felt his own. But the time for games was over.

"No more," he said, his voice raw with need. "Come to me, Jessie."

She stopped and faced him. Her arms rested at her sides. Her chest rose with ragged, uneven breaths.

Pale moonlight from the bay window slanted across her full breasts. "I know this sounds silly, but...I think...I'm nervous."

He knew why. This wasn't a careless gesture. This wasn't a kiss to be forgotten. This was something that would change both their lives radically. But did she know the depth or width of the impact it would have?

He doubted it. She'd lived her life conservatively, shielding her heart. Now she was about to take the biggest risk. He, too, felt as if he were on the edge of a precipice. Tension spiraled through him. *Are you sure about this, Brooks?* As sure as he could be.

"Me, too." He slid his knuckles along her cheek, curling his fingers around the nape of her neck. "But you don't have to be nervous with me. We'll take it nice and slow. Hell, we'll take all night if we have to."

She chuckled. "I thought you said you'd wait forever."

"I didn't say forever. I just said I would have waited a lot longer. Forever is asking too much. I'm not a saint. I'm just a man. A man who wants you...needs you...too much."

"Good." She draped her arms over his shoulders, lifting her leg to his hip and fitting her body snugly, intimately, against him. He caught her silky thigh with his hand and pressed his erection into the heat of her softness. "'Cause I don't think I could wait all night. I feel like I'm about to explode right now."

He nuzzled her neck, dipping his tongue into the hollow of her throat, feeling her pulse race along with his. "Demanding, aren't you."

"I know what I want." She clutched his shoulders and let her head fall back. "And I want you, Wade. I want you now. I need—"

"I know, baby. You've got me, Jess. Just hang on."

Bending, he lifted her into his arms and carried her to the bed. As he placed her on the thick comforter, she began tugging at his belt buckle. So much for slow and thorough. The temperature in the room shot up at least ten degrees. Jessie's soft moans filled his ears. Her kisses were urgent, her hands frenzied.

He let her set the pace for a few minutes, let her buck and squirm beneath him as he tried to kick off his pants. Then he straddled her, keeping his weight off her, and trapped her hands above her head.

"Hold still," he said through gritted teeth, not sure he could contain his desire much longer. "Don't move."

"What's wrong?"

"Nothing. Not one blessed thing."

Slowly he released her wrists, but she didn't move. He eased his hands down her arms, and she left them high above her head. He traced the curve of bone and flesh along her arms over her shoulders and across her chest until he took his time lavishing attention to her breasts. Cupping each one, he weighed the soft, firm mounds in his palm, flicking her nipples with his tongue, leaving a moist trail where his open mouth tasted her. His ragged breath fanned her heated skin, and he watched her nipples harden to stiff peaks.

She shifted restlessly beneath him, arching her back off the bed. "Wade..."

"I know, baby. I know." He suckled her breast, tugging, pulling at her until he heard her inhale harshly then release the breath on a hoarse moan. "This will make it better, so much better."

His hands encircled her small waist. Her skin was smooth as silk. He thought he could touch her forever and never grow bored or tired of discovering new things about her. Each caress, each exploration, uncovered something new and different, and elicited exciting reactions from her.

His fingers traced the slope of her belly, the dip of her navel, the soft plane sliding low to the black panty that barely covered her. He followed the delicate lace from her hip down to the core of her femininity. She was hot, moist, and more than ready for him.

"Wade, please..." Jessie clutched his shoulders, drove her fingers through his wavy hair, pulling him down to her. She thought she might implode if he didn't bring her to release.

In one swift move that left her breathless, he stripped off her panties, removing the last barrier between them. But he still didn't enter her.

He dismissed her anxious pleas and took his time, bringing her close to a climax then letting her settle back down to a simmering level. Again and again, he stirred her fires until she thought she would be consumed.

When she felt she couldn't endure one more moment, he finally covered her with his body, stretching his legs along hers until she wrapped her legs around his waist. Tugging on his hips, she felt his rigid heat push inside her. She arched her back, moaning with relief as her body stretched to accept him.

Again, he refused to go further. He settled his elbows on either side of her head and waited for her to meet his gaze. When she did, she felt the breath completely knocked out of her. Those deep-set, penetrating eyes shook her beyond reason. She realized in that moment that she had done the unthinkable. She had fallen in love with Wade Brooks.

Never would she have dreamed of feeling so much for a man or even admitting it to him! Did he sense the depth of her feelings already? His gaze was a mixture of blinding passion and infinite tenderness. She wanted him to know that this moment with him was different, far different than she'd ever imagined or experienced with anyone else.

"I—I've never felt like this before. Never experienced anything like this. I—I..." Her throat closed from fear or love she wasn't sure.

He cupped her face. "I know, Jessie. Scary, isn't it?"

"You were right. So right." She moaned and lifted her hips toward him, grinding herself against him, needing to feel more, to be closer, closer, closer.

"Nothing a man likes better than to be right."

"Nothing?" she teased.

He gave a slow, seductive smile. "Maybe this."

He kissed her until their bodies began to move as one, pushing faster, harder, pounding, pounding until her world shattered into brilliant shards of light. She heard him cry her name as his echoed through her heart.

He dipped his head against her shoulder and collapsed against her. She folded her arms around him, holding him close, cherishing each moment. For a long while they lay perfectly still, completely joined, exhausted, replete, at peace.

When she opened her eyes, Wade was there, looking at her, devouring her with his heated gaze.

"Don't leave me," he said, his voice rough with emotion.

"I won't. I couldn't." Because she loved him, as she'd loved no other. Was this, she wondered, how she knew he was her soul mate?

WADE'S APPETITE for Jessie was insatiable. It was as if he'd regressed in age back to his high school and college days. He couldn't get enough of her, tasting, touching, loving her until dawn broke and tendrils of light seeped into her bedroom.

The sheets were rumpled and pushed to the bottom of the bed. The rest of their clothes were banished to the floor or other parts of the house. Noticing chill bumps along her arms, he pulled what covers he could find over her limbs.

"Tired?" he asked.

"Exhausted," she said sleepily. "But delirious."

He smoothed her tousled hair off her brow and brushed a kiss across her swollen lips.

For the first time in years he felt at peace. Finally assured that she wasn't going to kick him out of her house, send him home or try to untangle herself from his life, he relaxed and let his eyes droop closed.

With every beat of his heart, he knew he loved Jessie. Cupid had struck for the second time in his life. This time, he decided, would be the last. But this time felt more intense, more desperate, more encompassing than the first.

Maybe it was because, with Tanya, he'd felt as though they had forever. But he'd learned how short and cruel life could be. He now knew the value of a day, a moment, a kiss. And he'd make each with Jessie take on the blessed sheen of the last.

He felt whole again. Loneliness vanished with Jessie in his arms. His heart felt complete, full, overflowing. Basking in the warmth of love, he wrapped his arms around her and fell into a deep, contented sleep.

JESSIE'S HAND RESTED over Wade's heart, where she wanted it to stay for an eternity. His slow, steady breaths reassured her. Never had she felt so safe. Never had she felt so cherished, so treasured. With Wade, she finally felt complete.

The struggle she'd been waging against men her entire life seemed to have died in Wade's arms. He made her feel accepted for who she was, what she wanted out of life. He wouldn't be the type to clip her wings or to try to transform her into something she wasn't. After all, he'd loved his wife. He'd allowed her the freedom Jessie needed. And she felt confident that he loved her now the same way she loved him.

With a contented smile, her skin tingling from head to toe with a warm glow, she settled against Wade's side and allowed herself, for the first time ever, to relax in the arms of a lover...and sleep.

WHEN HE BLINKED against the harsh sunlight pouring into the room, he glanced at the bedside table. The clock read twelve minutes after ten. Time had ceased to matter. Only Jessie did.

He began envisioning the day ahead, of them taking a long, leisurely shower, taking turns lathering each other between slow, heated kisses. Maybe they'd take a stroll through her neighborhood, go to brunch, spend the afternoon at a movie or swimming in his pool. He could see them kissing, holding hands, making love in the late afternoon and far into the night.

Jessie began to stir, her body rubbing languorously against his, like a cat stretching. His heart jumpstarted. He soothed his hand down her back. "Good morning."

"Hmm." She gave him a squeeze around the middle and snuggled closer. "How long have you been awake?"

"Not long."

She gave him a sleepy gaze. "You weren't watching me sleep or anything, were you?"

"Better than television." He kissed her nose. "I was planning our day."

"Yeah?" She smiled suggestively and ran her fingers over his chest. "I have a few ideas myself. Want to compare notes?"

He grinned. "You look beautiful, by the way."

"Sure. Without your glasses or contacts." She combed her fingers through her hair.

"I don't need glasses or contacts."

"You don't?" She pushed up onto her elbows. "But you wore glasses in your picture. On your book."

He rolled his eyes. "Publicity. They thought it made me look scholarly. But I meant you looked beautiful while you were sleeping."

She dipped her head into his shoulder. "God, I hope I didn't snore."

"Not too loudly."

Punching him playfully on the arm, she settled back into the warmth of his body. "So, what were your plans? A shower?"

He told her the things he'd imagined them doing together, adding a few risqué ideas as he nuzzled the side of her neck. "What's your pleasure?"

"You," she said, her voice husky.

Rolling her over until she lay on top of him, he explored her backside, enjoying the softness of her skin. "You've got me."

"Good." Her eyes brightened. "You know what this means, don't you?"

"What?"

"That I've won."

"Won?"

"Me?"

"The bet." She bent her head and nibbled at his neck and chest.

Her words blurred in his head, but the meaning slammed into his heart. "That's all you can think about now?"

"Well, no." She wiggled against the top of his thighs. "But it does cause one small problem."

He didn't want to hear any more. Was this fate's cruel joke, to make him love a woman who couldn't separate work from life? Jessie was exactly like Tanya. What the hell had he done?

He'd given in to the heat of the moment. He'd been reckless. Careless. A goddamn fool. That's what.

The air in the room grew thin and lifeless. His lungs compressed, burned. Unable to run. Unable to savor waking up with Jessie in his arms. A hard, unmistakable knot twisted inside him. Suddenly he felt trapped.

But not by Jessie. By his own weakness.

Shoving his fingers through his hair, he exhaled sharply.

*What now?*

"What's wrong?"

"Nothing." *Everything.* He sat up and she rolled off him.

"You're angry."

Jessie's picture should be in the dictionary beside the word "independent." She didn't want a relationship. She wanted to win a damn bet.

Well, she could have her work.

But he would have nothing. Not even his heart. Because he'd given it to Jessie last night.

His picture should be the definition for "fool."

As much as it had hurt, he'd let Tanya go off, find herself, conquer her career and kill herself in the process. And he would let Jessie go, as well. Wasn't that the ultimate gift of love?

Using every ounce of restraint, longing for solitude instead of the pain associated with love, he stood and pulled on his pants. He looked at the end of the bed for his shirt but only saw Jessie's discarded panties.

She pushed up onto her elbows, then sat straight, the sheet falling away from her, revealing her flushed breasts. "What are you doing?"

He checked the other side of the bed. No shirt. "Looking for my damn shirt."

"It's in the living room." Her tone sounded flat. But she looked disheveled, shaken.

"Oh, well..." He rubbed his hand over his chest. "I, um..." How could he say this? He couldn't just run like a coward. He had to tell her. Sitting on the edge of the bed, as far away from her as he could be, he forced himself to meet her wide gaze. "It won't work, Jessie."

"What won't?"

"This. Us. You and me."

She paled to the color of the ivory sheet. "But you said... I don't understand."

"Obviously. You have a lot to learn about relationships and love. This kind of thing isn't always right, or good, or best." He couldn't look at her. He stared at his hands, clasped between his knees. His gut twisted with doubt and that raw, aching pain he knew so well. If that was any indication, then he truly did love Jessie. But that didn't mean he was smart, or that it would work.

"Look," he said, "maybe we didn't jump into this. Or maybe we did. Maybe we were blinded by our need to be together. Maybe..."

"Just leave." Her mouth thinned. She jerked the sheet up to cover herself.

Couldn't she understand she was keeping them apart? This was her decision, not his. "Jess—"

"I was wrong."

"So was I." He stood, feeling awkward. His entire body ached, the pain resonating from his heart. "Jessie, can't you see we're not right for each other?"

"I can see a man who's afraid."

His shoulders snapped into place. "You're wrong."

But she wasn't. She was dead-on. He was scared. Frightened by the depth of emotion he felt for her. By his need to be with her. By his knowledge that she didn't need him as badly as he needed her. He'd never wanted to feel that way again.

"You want a woman who's a doormat," she said. "Someone to fetch your slippers and whip you up a delicious dinner. All without breaking a sweat or a nail. Someone who doesn't have a care in the world other than you and your needs. Well, that's not reality."

"You think every man is just like your father, don't you?"

"Don't analyze me. You're the one living in a dreamworld, Doc."

"No, you are, Jessie. Because you think love falls into neat little packages. But people fall in love. And that's what makes every situation unique with its own difficulties. You can't put people into your little categories. They don't work that way. I don't work that way. That's why your program won't work."

She jerked her chin. "You're right about one thing. I'm not the woman for you."

She took a ragged but calming breath. Shifting to the side of the bed, she pulled the sheet with her and stood, wrapping it around her like a long gown. "I always feared marriage and commitment required a sacrifice that I'd never be willing to make. I was right. The kind of sacrifice you're requiring would strip me of who I am, of my dignity, my very soul. If that's what a soul mate does, then I don't want one. I don't need you."

Her words cut Wade to the quick. But the pain they brought sharpened his focus. On the past, and on the present.

His marriage had been one-sided. Tanya had been selfish, never compromising, never giving, always taking. He'd bent over backward accommodating, chalking it up to giving love room to grow.

He could see the same thing happening with Jessie. He'd give; she'd take. It might not end in physical death, but it would end. And his heart would be destroyed all the same.

"You're right." Sadness resonated in his voice and made his limbs feel heavy with fatigue. "And I wouldn't ask that of you."

Maybe he had been living in a fairy tale, a fantasy world, where he could have a companion, what Jessie called a charm bracelet, where he didn't have to love too much, give too much, lose too much. It had been a defense mechanism to protect his heart.

Now, he saw his relationship with Jessie clearly. She'd effectively ripped away his barriers, leaving him exposed, vulnerable, and he could see what he really wanted—a full partner. Not a lopsided relationship, as his marriage had been.

Frankly, he wanted Jessie.

But the hard truth was, she didn't want him enough.

She wasn't about to make compromises or sacrifices to force their relationship to work. And he wouldn't bend over backward again, breaking his back and heart to make something impossible plausible.

"I'll get my shirt and go."

"Fine." She watched him, her eyes wary, guarded, her chest heaving.

He wanted to go to her, kiss her one last time, wrap his arms around her and tell her he knew how much it hurt. But it would only prolong the agony. He had to make a clean break. The sooner, the better.

"Goodbye, Jessie."

# 11

"WHERE THE HELL have you been?" Jack asked.

Jessie cringed but kept walking, right past his office. She knew she was late, more than three hours late, for their meeting. But after Wade had walked out of her life and heart, she hadn't been able to move. She'd barely been able to breathe. The last thing she needed this afternoon was the Spanish Inquisition.

"Any messages for me?" she called over her shoulder, giving her voice a cheerful lilt that defied every aching piece of her. She continued on toward the sanctity of her own office.

Work would heal her wounds.

In time.

Maybe that's how her mother had felt when her marriage ended. Maybe Jack had been right. Over the years her mother's advice had been accurate. For a brief time she'd put aside all her mother had taught her and tasted love and passion. But it had cost her dearly.

Each movement reminded her of the sweet loving she'd shared with Wade. Each beat of her heart reminded her of his rejection, the sharp twisting pain of reality.

Purposefully ignoring how her eyes burned from too many tears, how her lips felt swollen from Wade's kisses, she settled into her chair and clicked on her computer. She'd take care of payroll first. Then she had a bounced check from a new client to handle. Sometime she had to face her computer program. Maybe she'd simply start pairing up clients and hope for the best. Wasn't that what Jack did with his theory?

"You look like you could use this," Jack said, following her into her office and setting a mug of coffee on her desk.

"That bad, huh?" She tried a smile but it was weak and limp.

His brow furrowed with concern. "Want to tell me about it?"

"Not really." She clicked her mouse and pulled up the financial data on Sole Mates. "Were there any messages?"

"Were you expecting someone specific to call?"

She heard the silent question and her nerves unraveled. She wanted to be left alone in her misery. She didn't want sympathy, or pity or advice. She simply wanted to get on with her life. And forget Wade.

"I just wanted to know if anyone, that means any person, male, female, Mother, Father, anyone at all called for me. If so, then do I need to call them back?" She felt her blood pressure spike.

His startled gaze had a worldly understanding. Not of pity or sympathy but of empathy.

She sighed. "I'm sorry. That outburst wasn't called for."

"Would have helped if I'd answered your question in the first place." He stretched his long frame into the chair across from her desk and templed his fingers over his chest. "No one called here asking specifically for you. Don't worry about anything. I handled everything."

"Thanks, I appreciate it."

"Not a problem. We're a team, remember?" He tapped his fingers against his chin. "When you check your messages at home, you'll find several."

Damn, why had she turned off her ringer? Because she'd needed to be alone, completely alone, without any interruptions. Now, she desperately needed constant and relentless distractions. "From?"

"Me."

She gave him a questioning look.

"Hey, I'm not going to pry. Whatever happened is your business. Not mine." He gave a slight shrug that reminded her of when they'd first become friends in college. He was treading on delicate turf. "But I was worried. You have to admit it's unusual for you not to be here at the crack of dawn. And it's after three now."

At one time in her life she would have been defensive, irritated, but somehow today his concern touched her. "I know. I'm sorry. I should have called."

He waved off her apology. "I never do. And you don't complain. I was just worried." He gave her a comforting smile. "I am your big brother."

"By two minutes."

"Doesn't change the way things are. Those two minutes give me the right to worry about my little sister."

His big brother routine tugged on her sense of humor. Her mouth crooked into a semblance of a smile. "I'm okay."

"You sure?"

"No. But I will be. Eventually." It would just take time, maybe a long time. But she would get over Wade. She had no choice.

"I'm here if you want to talk."

"I know and I appreciate it. Maybe later." She shifted her gaze back to the computer, anxious to switch topics. If she were to discuss Wade now, she'd end up blubbering like an idiot.

Jack gave a curt nod. "Okay, then. Now, sit back and let me tell you what I've been doing all day."

Swiveling her chair to face him again, she propped her arms on her desk. "Why does that worry me?"

"It shouldn't. I've been making you a fortune."

Her eyebrows lifted. "I like the sound of that."

"I've landed on the perfect marketing ploy for Sole Mates's official launch."

"So this isn't money I can put in the bank right away, is it?"

"Actually, it's probably going to cost you first."

"Of course. Better let me have my coffee." She sipped the dark brew, which tasted tart, almost abrasive, as if it had been made hours ago. She felt the hot liquid burn its way into her empty stomach and kick her brain into gear. "Okay, let me have it."

"What do most of our customers want out of Sole Mates?" he asked.

"A soul mate."

"Yes, but..."

"Was that a trick question?"

He shook his head. "It's so obvious. What do you do with a soul mate?"

She really didn't want to think about that one this afternoon, not after she'd just lost hers.

That gave her heart a jolt. Was Wade her soul mate? Part of her thought so. Part of her didn't want to believe it. Maybe finding one's soul mate was like searching for the Fountain of Youth. It was a myth, a dream. Not reality.

And if soul mates really existed, then Wade couldn't be hers. Not when he couldn't accept her for who she was, for what she wanted. That made them incompatible, opposite poles of soul mates.

But it had felt so right, so incredibly right.

Confused by the questions spinning around her head, she rested her chin in her hand. Anguish pinched her heart. "I don't know what soul mates do. Live the rest of their lives together?"

Jack gave a low growl. "As what?"

She frowned. "As lovers? As man and—"

He snapped his fingers. "Exactly. Man and...and..."

"Wife." She ground the word out between her teeth. The headache she'd been nursing all day blasted into a full-blown migraine. A sharp pain hit her behind one eyeball, making it feel as if it had been set on fire.

"Yes!" His eyes sparkled with excitement. He stood and began pacing. "And how do you get to be man and wife?"

She pressed her fingers against her closed eyes. "Couldn't you just tell me the idea instead of making me do all the work, Jack?"

"Sure you're okay?" His voice softened.

She wanted to quit playing games. "Jack, just tell me."

"Okay, here goes." He clapped his hands together, and she winced. "A wedding. Every one of our customers would love to have Sole Mates lead to their wedding. Right?"

"Well, I don't know. Is there a rule that soul mates have to marry? Or could they just live together as significant others?"

He frowned. "A wedding."

"Okay, a wedding." Why did saying that word make her heart feel empty, like a deep, dark void?

"Our official launch or grand opening will be a wedding."

"Who's getting married? You?" Certainly not her. That reality brought a distinct pang to her heart.

"No one. We don't need a real wedding. This will be a mock one. One that will highlight Sole Mates." Jack settled one hip on the edge of her desk. "We can hire an actress and actor to be the honorary bride and groom. The reception will be a grand affair with champagne, a wedding cake, a band."

She fingered her temple again. "The cost is rising."

"Come on, you love it."

"I'm not in love with anything." Or anyone. She couldn't keep the grief from her voice. Still, the topic gave her something to focus on. Something besides Wade. But did it have to be a wedding? The very thing she'd started to envision with Wade?

Pushing aside her personal feelings, ready to latch on to any idea that could take over her thoughts and block out her pain, she added, "But I will admit I'm intrigued. What will we do? Send out invitations?"

"Exactly. Wedding invitations. Except it will look totally legit. Not like an ad or promo. Who the bride and groom are will be a surprise."

Amazed at Jack's plan, she leaned back in her chair. Her pulse thrummed. "And when the guests arrive, they'll realize it's to launch Sole Mates."

"Right! We can give away a free membership or two."

"Good idea," she said, ready to jump in and swim with this new idea. At least she could forget Wade.

Temporarily. "Whoever catches the bridal bouquet and the garter will get free memberships."

Jack laughed. "Perfect. I'll bet you'll have singles jumping all over each other to catch them."

She gave a wry grin. "Better than the last wedding I attended when none of the singles wanted to catch either. Didn't you let the garter bounce right off you?"

"And you let the bouquet fall to the floor."

That had been then. She had a strange feeling, if faced with the same situation, she'd clutch the bouquet to her heart and look for Wade.

"NO, NO, NO," Jessie said the following day. She slid her chair back and met her brother's challenging stare. "You can't say it that way. Sounds all wrong. Too confusing."

"How would you do it?"

"Not that way."

He flung the mock invitation at her. "Do it better, then."

"Fine." She grabbed a pen, poised it over the scribbled attempts that had been scratched through. "If our names are on the invitation, it's a dead giveaway. If we want the wedding to be a surprise then..."

Edgy, she tapped her pen against the desktop. "What if we make it simple, straightforward." She began writing. "We'll list the date and time the wedding will begin. Then the place—the ballroom at the Crescent Hotel."

"Okay," Jack said, crossing his arms over his chest, "but that doesn't solve the problem of the bride and groom's identity."

"Give me a second," she said. "Then we'll say...'to protect the innocent bride and groom from the paparazzi or press, their identity has been withheld and will be revealed at the time of the wedding.'" She jotted down more notes on the paper. "We can add something about 'when responding with your reply, please use discretion and keep this invitation a secret.'"

Jack chuckled. "Yeah right. Every guest will blab."

"Exactly," she said, laying the pen on the desk. "Which will provide us with more publicity. There will be a definite buzz going around Dallas as speculation accumulates."

He tapped her on the brow. "You know, sis, I like the way you think."

Relieved, she returned his smile. One of the first genuine ones she'd felt since she'd lost Wade. But thinking of him now made her smile waver. "Thanks. I'll call in the order for the invitations this afternoon. It should take a week to get them back."

He nodded. "When they arrive, why don't you bring them by my apartment and we'll make a night of licking and stamping?"

"Best invitation I've had recently." Her statement was meant to be funny but it struck a raw nerve inside her.

Jack's gaze narrowed. "You interested in finding a date, sis?"

She bristled. "Definitely not. So don't get any ideas. Just keep your eyes off my shoes. I'm not in the market."

Rubbing his hands down his thighs, Jack said, "Whatever you want." He grabbed a legal pad and glanced over their to-do list. "What about the guests?"

"The list is coming together. I've culled several mailing lists of singles in the Dallas area, cross-

matched their single status with their financial
bracket, which eliminated several thousand, thankfully, and am printing out the final list. I should have
all the numbers this afternoon."

"Good." He moved the chair beside him and
propped his bare feet onto it. "We also need to make
sure we've added any personal friends and, of course,
our current clients."

"Definitely." Jessie typed into the computer their
sample invitation. "Just give me your list to add to the
master."

"Will do." He cut his eyes toward her. "What about
Wade?"

That snagged her attention. Her pulse accelerated.
Her heart constricted.

Jack gave her a penetrating look that made her
stomach free-fall. "What are you going to do about
him?"

"Wade?" she asked, trying to sound nonchalant
even though her hands trembled. "Wade Brooks?
What about him?"

"Are you going to invite him?"

It seemed simple on the surface, but complicated
deep in her heart. Only one possible answer surfaced.
"No."

"Isn't he consulting for us?"

"Was. Believe me, he wouldn't want to come." She
pushed out of her chair and left the office before she
revealed more than she cared to. But she couldn't
shake the feeling of Jack's speculative gaze following
after her.

WADE TIPPED A BEER bottle against his mouth and took
a long, hard pull, downing half the contents in a single

swallow. "You ever go out to the tracks, Jack?" He pointed toward the television with the end of the bottle. "Put a little money on your favorite horse?"

"Once in a while." Jack lay stretched out on his sofa, his bare feet propped on the armrest. "It's a dangerous pastime."

"So is your business." He watched the thoroughbreds charging around the last bend and racing for the finish line, but his mind wasn't on betting, making, or losing money. It was on Jessie.

Where was she? What was she doing? Was she missing him as desperately as he missed her? Did any of it matter anymore? It had been one week since they'd made love, since he'd realized his mistake, since he'd lost her. It seemed more like a decade had passed with endless, sleepless nights and dark, dreary days.

"What's so dangerous about dating?"

Wade lifted a heavy brow. His whole body felt weighted down. But he knew he wasn't sick. It was an emotional symptom of the pain roiling through his gut. He could rationally understand why he was feeling so miserable. But all the rationale, intelligence and psychoanalysis couldn't take away the dull ache in his heart. "You obviously haven't ever been in love."

"I wouldn't say that." Jack popped the top off another beer. "In fact, I've been thinking more and more about the possibility."

"Not with that secretary of yours?"

Jack laughed. "Gotta let that kind go. But with Amber..." He grinned. "It might be the biggest mistake of my life if I were to do that. Maybe my sister has rubbed off on me."

"Jessie? What do you mean?"

"She's contemplating the same thing."

Those words skewered his heart. Jessie was seeing someone else? Loving someone else? Had she rebounded from him right into someone else's arms? His world collapsed around him.

"I know I make it sound easy. In a way, it's the easiest thing I've ever done." Jack took a pull on his beer. "Before, I always found the girl I was dating somebody she liked better."

"Never made you jealous?"

"Not once. That told me it wasn't right. But with Amber..." He clenched his fist. "She's mine."

Wade wished he could think the same thing about Jessie. Fact was, she wasn't his. Never had been.

"In the past, the other women forgot all about me when faced with a real prospect for love and marriage."

"Maybe you can do that," Wade said with a humorless grin, "but for some of us—" he brushed his fingertips against a make-believe lapel "—no one else would ever compare."

Jack threw the silver cap from his beer at Wade. It landed with a polite thud on his chest. "You know, Brooks, maybe my sister was right about you."

Wade flinched. For the first time in the two hours since he'd arrived at Jack's apartment to kick back and enjoy the afternoon watching the horse races, Wade lifted his head from the leather chair. Hell, he hadn't even bothered to dress in anything more than running shorts, an old college T-shirt and tennis shoes. But there was nothing casual about the glance he shot Jack. "What did she say about me?"

The doorbell prevented Jack from answering. He

groaned as he pushed himself up from the couch. "Probably one of your groupies tracking you down."

"Or one of your old flames, wanting you to find her Mr. Right," Wade mumbled, sipping on his beer. His mood turned morose as his thoughts settled on Jessie again. For the last week he'd been miserable, when setting her free should have brought relief.

She wasn't the settling-down type. She didn't want marriage. She wasn't the type to make sacrifices, which a relationship required. When he thought of Jessie, he thought of her only in terms of forever and ever.

Jack opened the door. "Yes?"

"They're here!" A breathless Jessie stood in the doorway, her hair tousled by the summer breeze, her cheeks red from too-much sun, her eyes bright as jewels. "You ready for a little licking and—"

Her gaze collided with Wade's. His heart slammed against his breastbone. Immediately, he sat up, combed his fingers through his tousled hair and pushed to his feet. Damn. Why hadn't he anticipated this? Why hadn't Jack told him his sister might drop by?

"Hello, Jessie," he said, his voice sounding rougher than he wished.

She stood immobile, frozen halfway inside the door. She wore a tank top and running shorts. He'd never seen her dressed so casually, except for the last time, when she'd been draped in a sheet. Which brought back burning memories and jagged pain.

"Come on in," Jack encouraged her.

"I didn't know you had company." She spoke to her brother, but her gaze remained stuck on Wade. Her hand clutched a shopping bag at her side. "I—I, uh, should have called."

"Hey, it's no big deal." Jack held the door open, unable to close it with his sister still standing in the doorway.

"You two probably have business to discuss." Wade grabbed his keys off the coffee table. Part of him wondered if this was fate. Should he say something to her? Apologize? Beg for another chance? Or was he being foolish to want her, to need her so desperately? When she didn't need him. When she'd found someone else. His throat cinched tight. "I'll be going."

"You stay," Jessie said, her voice thick, her gaze accusing "I'll come back later."

"Why don't you both stay?" Jack said. "We'll order pizza."

Both Jessie and Wade ignored him. He felt electricity charge the air between them. Where once it had been desire, red-hot passion, now he sensed anger emanating from Jessie. Why should she be furious with him? He'd only spared them both heartache. She wouldn't have wanted to commit to him. Would she?

Doubts assailed him. But he was too confused, too unnerved by Jessie, by the thought of her with someone else, to sort through his jumbled thoughts. He needed space. He needed time alone to figure out his feelings.

"Jack, I'll see you on the green Friday," Wade said. He stopped a couple of feet short of Jessie and waited for her to move out of his way.

"Sure. Okay."

"Jessie." He felt a contraction in his heart. What could he say to bridge the gap dividing them. Was it only pride? Or destiny?

She stepped to the side to let him pass. "Wade."

He couldn't move, couldn't take his eyes off her. The pain in her blue-green eyes held him transfixed. *Tell her, Brooks. Tell her how you feel. It doesn't matter if it doesn't make sense. It doesn't matter if it seems impossible. Doesn't love make all things possible?*

No. He knew all too well the answer to that. Love wasn't a cure-all. It sure couldn't alleviate the pain inside his heart.

Jessie gave him a pointed look as she grasped the door handle. "Are you going to air-condition all of Texas?"

He gave a terse nod of goodbye and walked through the door and out of Jessie's life. It was her way of dismissing him. Of dismissing all they'd shared. It was probably for the best. Then why did it hurt so damn much?

"So, YOU WANT TO TELL ME what that was all about?"

"Not particularly." Jessie put the sack of invitations on Jack's kitchen table. "Mind if I have a beer?"

"Make yourself at home."

"Thanks." She pulled out several boxes of printed invitations. They looked like the real thing in ecru white with a beveled edge and curlicue fancy printing.

Staring at them, reading over them for accuracy, she felt a sharp jab to her heart. She sniffed away her strange mood and grabbed a beer out of Jack's fridge. What was she doing wanting her own wedding invitations? Had she lost her mind? Marriage was the last thing she wanted.

So was Wade.

She could get over him. It would have been easier if she hadn't seen him today. But even if she never saw

him again, she knew the pain in her heart would remain acute. "Want me to order a pizza?" She began
sorting out the envelopes, reply cards, invitations and
tissue paper, setting up an assembly line. "Looks like
it's going to be a long night."

"Sure, go ahead." Jack swung a chair around and
straddled it. "I've got Ben & Jerry's ice cream in the
freezer and possibly a hunk of Valentine's chocolate
somewhere. We can make a pigfest."

Settling one fist on her hip, she met his amused
gaze. "What are you talking about?"

"Isn't it obvious? This depression you're in."

"I am not depressed."

He gave a coarse laugh. "And it's not about Wade,
either."

She refused to look at him, refused to acknowledge
his perception. Sometimes she loved the bond they
shared. Sometimes it simply annoyed her. "Let's get
busy with these invitations."

Jack tapped an envelope against the edge of the table, jarring her nerves. "Whatever you say, sis."

# 12

DUMBSTRUCK, Wade stared at the invitation that he'd pulled from his mailbox. A surprise wedding? A secret bride and groom? Was this a joke? A prank?

Confused, he turned over the thick envelope and stared at the return address. It didn't have a name, only a street address. But he recognized it as Jessie's.

Heat seared his insides. His hand closed into a fist, crumpling the envelope. He glared at the invitation as if it were offensive, repulsive, ugly.

But it wasn't. It was printed on expensive paper, the bold black slashes were elegant, tasteful. It wasn't gaudy. It was beautiful. If this was a joke, someone had spent a lot of money.

What the hell was going on?

Had Jessie concocted a prank? After all, she had stormed into his shower the day they'd first met. What would make him think she wouldn't do something as bizarre as send him a fake wedding invitation?

Or was he simply trying not to face an alarming possibility? Had she suddenly decided to get married to someone else? Tension twisted his stomach into a knot.

He skimmed the "please use discretion" line and wondered if she'd found someone famous. But who? He hadn't heard anything, other than Jack had hinted she was serious with someone. Had it gone from serious to terminal that fast?

If she was getting married, then this could be the quickest rebound in history. If she'd changed her "I'm not interested in love and romance" line, then it was quick enough to give him whiplash. And second thoughts.

There had to be a good explanation. Maybe the invitation was for Jack and Amber. Maybe Jessie was so ruthless and determined to win that bet with Jack that she'd computer-matched herself with another client at Sole Mates. He had to get to the bottom of it. Immediately.

Reaching for the phone, he dialed her number, and began pacing as he counted each unanswered ring. His heart beat loud in his ears. Finally, after six rings, the answering machine picked up. He disconnected the call and tried her office.

"Sole Mates. Can I help you?" a perky voice answered.

"I need to speak with Jessie."

"May I tell her who's calling?"

"No." He wasn't about to take the chance that she'd refuse his call. "I want to speak with her. This is important."

"Well, if you don't tell me who it is, then I can't leave a message, can I? She's not available at the moment."

Of course she'd set up a blockade around herself. Damn.

"Is Jack in?" Wade gritted his teeth.

"Yeah, sure. He's always available. Hold on."

Wade waited a few seconds before Jack answered. He cut right to the chase. "So what's this invitation?"

"You got it, eh?" Jack sounded upbeat, enthusiastic.

"What does it mean? Are you and Amber...?"

"Not yet." Jack cleared his voice. "It's pretty self-evident, isn't it?"

"Dammit, Jack. Is she? Is Jessie the..." His throat constricted. "...the...you know, the bride?"

"Now, Wade, I can't really talk about it. You'll find out all in good time. Are you going to come?"

"Tell me this," he said, ignoring the question, unwilling to contemplate that scenario. "Did Jessie send me the invitation? Or did you?"

Jack hesitated before he answered. "I did."

Why did that knowledge cut him to the quick? "So she doesn't know."

"No."

Wade circled his couch. "Is she in the office? Can I talk to her?"

"I really don't think that's a good idea, buddy. You're not exactly on her 'A' list these days. Give her some time."

How much time? And was time running out? Why did he care so damn much?

He stared at the date on the invitation. One week away. What could he do to stop her?

Nothing. This was her decision. She didn't even want him to know!

Clunking the phone into the receiver, he plopped onto the couch. There was nothing he could do. If she was getting married, then he'd have to live with it. No matter how much it crushed him.

THE WEEK SAILED BY in a torrential downpour of activities and last minute preparations. All of the nitpicky details required Jessie's constant attention. It was draining. But a relief. For it left her little time to dwell on her broken heart or thoughts of Wade.

It was nearly four o'clock on the day of the grand opening when Jessie managed to take a deep breath.

"There you are!" Jack said, striding down the long carpeted hallway in the Crescent Hotel. He readjusted his cummerbund on his tuxedo.

Jessie sat on a couch outside the main ballroom, her checklist securely in her lap, her cell phone nearby. "I've been here all day. Where have you been?"

"Got a late start, then I had trouble finding a tux." He gave a growl at the back of his throat as he tugged on his bow tie.

"Well, you look nice," she said. "The florist just finished, and the cake has arrived. The caterer is setting up the rest of the stations and tables."

He glanced at his watch. The subtle lighting made his hair glint like spun gold and the stark white of his collar showed off his bronze tan. "Guests should begin arriving in the next thirty minutes."

"Do you think we're ready?" she asked, trailing her finger down the checklist to see if she'd missed anything.

"Not yet. But we will be. Soon as you get dressed."

She glanced at her plain skirt. "You're right. I left my clothes in my car. I'll be back in a few minutes."

"Don't worry about your dress. You're going to have to wear something else."

Jessie frowned. "Why?" She read the grim lines around Jack's mouth. "What's happened?"

"The bride I hired didn't show. I called the agency and they don't know where the actress is."

Her hand folded around the cell phone as she lifted

it to her ear. "Couldn't they send somebody else over? Another model or actress?"

"Not at this late date. It's nearly five on a Saturday, Jess. I'm not sure we'd want somebody they could get, anyway. She might look like Danny DeVito."

She began to understand where Jack was going with this. And she wasn't going to do it. No way. Not in this lifetime. "Maybe that would help us. People would think if we could find a husband for a woman who looks like Danny DeVito then we could find a soul mate for anyone." She gave him a cocky grin. "Hey, maybe we could even use that as a slogan."

Jack's eyebrows slanted into a frown.

"Okay," she said, understanding his pointed silence. "But we signed a contract with that agency. They should—" she located the agency's phone number on her list and punched in the numbers "—bend over backward to find us a replacement."

He grabbed the phone out of her hand. "We don't have time. The guests will be arriving soon."

"What bride hasn't been a little late the day of her wedding? The guests will understand. It'll build more hype, more anticipation."

"Jess, you have to do it."

No. There had to be another way. She just had to think of it first. "No way."

"It's just for one day. Maybe it's for the best anyway. It will keep the spotlight on Sole Mates."

"Are you kidding? I'm not going to dress up like a bride." She almost spat the word, but only she knew how it brought a slicing pain to her heart.

"I didn't say you had to marry anybody."

"No, Jack, I won't—"

"Come on, Jess." He grabbed her arm and pulled

her off the couch. With a steady hand at her back, he urged her toward the bride's room across the hall, and the rented wedding dress waiting inside. "You can do this."

"Jack—"

"What choice do we have?" He opened the door.

Jessie came to a complete halt. Across the room, draped over a satin hanger, a beautiful sequined wedding dress glimmered like stardust in the sunlight pouring through the arched windows.

With his hand still at the base of her back, he gave her a slight push into the room. "I'll send Amber in when she arrives to help you get dressed."

The door clicked shut behind her. A deafening roar filled her ears. She stared at the dress for the longest time. Minutes seemed like microseconds as thoughts and visions spun around her mind. A tremor of revulsion—no, heartache—rocked through her. Tears burned the backs of her eyes, stinging reminders of all that would never be.

She'd never be a real bride, not with Wade as her groom. He'd taken the first chance for escape and run hell-bent away from commitment. Could it have really been his anger over her wanting to work on the program? Was that the real problem? Or was he simply looking for an escape route?

Maybe she wasn't the marrying type. Maybe she wasn't meant to be a bride. Well, she wouldn't even be one today! She wouldn't even get a pretend ceremony. They were going to jump right to the reception after the guests had filed into the ballroom and the bride and groom appeared and made the announcement that this was the grand opening of Sole Mates.

Her throat closed tight. She was doomed to be single. At one time being single had been acceptable to her. She'd wanted to be alone. To be single. Forever. Until she'd met Wade. And he'd changed everything.

She'd started to imagine Wade as her groom! The thought that once would have been laughable was now heartbreaking. She felt the crack widen inside her chest and break apart her hopes and dreams. She'd never walk down a red velvet-lined aisle toward her waiting groom. Never make those lifelong vows. She'd always be alone. Because if she couldn't have Wade she didn't want a replacement. No man could make her feel the way he had.

But he'd rejected her. Blamed it on her! Over the past weeks she'd realized one simple fact: he still loved his first wife. She could never compete with a ghost. She wouldn't even try.

And she'd never make a fool of herself again. Not over love.

"WHAT ARE YOU DOING, Brooks?" Wade's hands gripped the steering wheel as he pressed harder on the accelerator. "This is a mistake."

But he couldn't stop himself. He couldn't turn the car around. He sped through yellow lights and around sluggish drivers.

*Five o'clock.* The time limit echoed like a gong crashing against his skull, making his temples throb and allowing a tension headache to seize the back of his neck like a vise. The wedding would begin at five o'clock. He glanced at the digital clock on the dash—4:55. Dammit.

He skirted around another car.

He had to make it on time.

He had to stop Jessie from marrying...someone... anyone but him!

"LAST BUTTON," Amber said.

Jessie felt as if she'd been sewn into a dress two sizes too small. She could barely take a breath. But she wasn't sure if the reason was the dress or the fact that she couldn't get Wade out of her mind and heart.

He still loved his first wife. That's the only reason she could fathom as to why he would hightail it away from her. He didn't want a soul mate. He didn't want to feel anything anymore. He only wanted a companion.

At one time she'd wanted a no-strings type of relationship, too, but not anymore. Not now that she'd had one brief moment with the man she knew had been made specifically for her.

Circling to stand beside the mirror, Amber's eyes grew round and dewy. "You're beautiful. Like a real bride."

But she wasn't a real bride. She'd never be.

Jessie rolled her bottom lip inward, biting it to keep the tears from consuming her. She gave herself a once-over in the mirror. The dress was as formfitting as they came. Every centimeter was covered in sparkling white sequins, shimmering and glittering with each tiny breath she took.

"This is just the type of dress I'd want," Amber said, "if I were to tie the knot." The wistful starry-eyed look in her friend's eyes worried Jessie. Oh, no. Had Jack broken Amber's heart?

"How are you and Jack doing?" she asked, hoping her brother hadn't dumped Amber as he had all the others. But if anyone could survive a broken heart, Amber could. *If only I could, too!*

"Oh, Jess!" Tears welled in Amber's eyes.

Automatically she reached for her friend, ready to offer a comforting shoulder and listening ear. At least now they'd have something else in common besides their careers. They could commiserate together.

"We're getting married!"

"What?" Jessie stared at Amber, stunned, shocked beyond belief.

Her friend gave her a quick, exuberant hug. "I'm not supposed to say anything yet. Jack proposed last night and thought we should wait until tonight to make the announcement. But I wanted you to know first."

"Amber, I'm so..." Stunned. She struggled to find the right word within her heart. "So...happy for you." She embraced the woman who would be her sister-in-law.

"Can you believe this?" Amber sniffed and laughed. "I always said I'd never marry, but when you meet the right man..."

*Yeah, when you meet the right man, your heart gets shattered.*

"Are you okay?" Amber asked, curling her stockinged toes into the carpet.

Yes. No. She couldn't explain her tumultuous emotions. If she started to discuss Wade, she'd crumple into a pile of sequins and sob. "I can't breathe very well."

"I should say not. But it's worth the sacrifice. Every man out there will be drooling over you and rushing to sign up for Sole Mates."

A quick rap on the door made them turn as Nina

Hart stepped into the room. "Well, Jack told me, but I couldn't believe it. Not until this moment."

Her mother walked toward her, her eggshell silk skirt whispering with each step. Were those tears welling in her eyes? "You're stunning."

Suddenly, Jessie couldn't hold back the emotions storming her heart. Her chest ached. She shuddered with a suppressed sob.

"What is it, Jess?" Amber reached forward.

But her mother's arms came around her first. Jessie couldn't answer. Tears clogged her throat.

"Are you upset by...my news?" Amber asked.

"What news?" Nina prodded.

The two women exchanged glances, making a silent pact to keep the engagement a secret awhile longer. Jess couldn't push any words past the lump in her throat.

"Love," her mother finally surmised. "Jack was right, wasn't he?"

She nodded. "I shouldn't have fallen for him. It was stupid. You warned me, Mother. I should have known better. I should have listened to you."

"Not Wade?" Amber said.

"Yes, Wade." Jessie sniffed. "How did you know?"

"Everyone knows." Amber handed her a tissue. "It's so obvious the way you look at each other."

"So, why all these tears, Jess?" her mother asked.

"Because it didn't work out. It *can't* work out."

"Why not?"

"Because...he doesn't want me." It was complicated but that was what it boiled down to.

Nina frowned and brushed a lock of Jessie's hair off her forehead. "I thought I taught you not to give up. If

Wade is the man you want, then you have to fight for him."

"But, Mother, I thought you didn't believe in love."

"Where did you get that idea?"

"My whole life!"

"Love gave you and Jack to me. Love also set me free to pursue my own life, reach my own potential. I just didn't want you to sacrifice your career for a man. You can have both."

"But you chose not to," she argued.

"I chose to focus on you and my career. Both were a full-time job. But I dated. Discreetly. I'm not a nun. And, please don't tell Jack, but the man he wants to set me up with...well, we've been seeing each other steadily for over a year now."

"Mother!" Jessie's jaw gaped. She'd never seen her mother as a full woman. Only as a caricature, until now.

Nina gave her an affectionate squeeze. She dabbed at Jessie's tears with her handkerchief. "Now, don't cry over this Wade. Just get him back."

*Get him back.* A new strength surged within Jessie. Was it possible? Could she fight for Wade and win him? Could she convince him to love again, to love her, that their love could work?

A bubble of laughter surged within her. Maybe it was possible. Who would have believed she could have chased down a reluctant love doctor in a shower stall? With love, anything was possible.

If Jack hadn't walked in that very minute to tell her it was time, Jessie would have bolted out of the hotel in search of Wade. As soon as the grand opening was over, she would.

Jack's eyes rounded. He gave a low whistle. "Sis, you're...you're..."

"Can't think of anything bad enough to say? Let's get this over with," she mumbled as she walked the only way she could in the narrow skirt—in baby steps.

"Wow!" he finally said.

"Yeah, yeah. You say that to all the brides you're not forced to marry."

"I mean it." He held out his arm for her.

"Amber told me, big brother," she whispered, and looped her arm through his. "Congrats. I hope you two will be very happy."

"Thanks, Jess." He gave his fiancée a wink.

"You'll do anything to win a bet, won't you?" Jessie accused.

"I'm not like you, Jess." He grinned. "Now, we just have to get you and Mother hitched."

Jessie gave her mother a watery, conspiratorial smile. Nina reached over, squeezed her hand, then handed her the bridal bouquet. The sweet smell of the blossoms tormented her. She felt her heart contract. She would get Wade back. Somehow. Someday.

"Come on," Jack said, tucking her arm close to his body. "I'm going to be your groom for the evening. I sent the actor home. That'll save us another expense. Let's throw the bouquet first. We'll give away a free membership to one woman then. Later, after we've cut the cake, we'll toss the garter. You did put on the garter, didn't you?"

She gave a slight nod, her throat constricted by too many emotions. Her groom...her Wade...wouldn't re- move the garter from her thigh. Her brother would! She groaned inwardly. Perfect. Just perfect. Could life get much worse? "Let's get this show on the road."

The sooner they started the party, the sooner they could get it over with and she could make a plan for getting Wade back into her life. Where he belonged.

SWEAT DAMPENING HIS SHIRT, Wade skidded to a halt outside the main ballroom. He curled his hand around the brass handle. He was late. The ceremony must already have started by now. So the only option he had left was to make a scene.

With his heart pummeling his breastbone, he yanked open the door. Stunned, he stared at the sea of people. It looked as if the ceremony had already concluded. Had they started early? Had it been the shortest ceremony on record? His pulse raced.

Then he saw her. Dressed in a waterfall of white shimmering sequins, she stood beneath a flowered arch. His gut contracted as if he'd been sucker punched.

Smiling like a radiant bride, she climbed onto a raised platform, several men offering her their helping hands, and waved her bridal bouquet. Squealing with laughter, the women in the crowd surged forward.

His heart stopped as things began to make sense. He was too late. Too damn late. Jessie was married. Married! To someone else. And he'd let it happen.

Without thinking, he pushed his way through the crowd, stalking toward Jessie. His eyes burned. His teeth clenched.

Then her gaze collided with his. She froze, her arm in midair. He couldn't tell if the intense blue of her eyes radiated anger, hatred or love. But he couldn't stop himself. His hands closed into fists as he anticipated meeting her groom. Who the hell was he?

A hush fell over the crowd as he made his way to

the platform. He took the steps two at a time until he reached her. His chest heaved with each breath.

"How could you do this?" Anger made his voice harsh. "How could you make love to me? How could you have said all you did? And all the while you were planning a wedding?"

"I wasn't planning the wedding while you and I...while we were..." A hot blush stole along her chest, neck and face.

"You said you didn't want marriage. You didn't want commitment."

"I changed my mind."

"How...how could you have...been with me, then turned around and married someone else?"

She gave a lift of one shoulder. "It was a spur-of-the-moment thing."

"I don't understand. Didn't you feel what I felt? Didn't you—"

"What should it matter to you?" she asked, her voice cool as the sculpted ice swan. "You didn't want me. You made that perfectly clear."

Mindless of the stares of everyone around them, he pushed up the sleeves of his shirt. "Where is this man you couldn't wait to marry? The one you were too embarrassed to put on the wedding invitation?"

A flitting smile tugged at the corner of her mouth.

Great, Wade thought, he'd probably just challenged someone like Arnold Schwarzenegger to a fight. But it didn't matter. Jessie was worth a broken nose...or arm...or leg. He'd fight to his last breath to keep her. He scanned the audience. "Where the hell is he?"

Jessie gave a soft laugh. Finally she understood what was happening. Wade thought she was really married. And he was jealous! Jealousy meant only one thing—he had to love her, too.

He loved Jessie.

As no one had ever loved her before.

She realized fear had overwhelmed him. Fear was something she could understand—she'd been afraid of an intimate relationship her entire life. But now that she'd experienced it with Wade, she wasn't afraid anymore. And she'd help him over this hurdle. Because she wasn't about to let him get away. But she had to make sure they'd have an equal partnership, not a one-sided relationship.

"Wade," she said, "you've got it all wrong. This isn't a wedding. It's a celebration."

His brow crinkled with confusion.

"This is to celebrate the grand opening of Sole Mates."

"Sole Mates?" he asked, his voice hollow.

"Yes, remember? Our company?" She took a step forward, no longer afraid of rejection, no longer afraid of anything, not with Wade back in her life. "This isn't a real wedding. I don't have a groom."

"But you're all dressed..." His gaze was like an intimate caress, one that heated her blood and tightened her breasts.

"Yes. Like a bride." She put her hand on his arm and felt his muscles contract. "But I'm without a groom. Are you volunteering for the position?"

Someone in the crowd gasped. Somebody else chuckled. Then an awkward silence followed.

Her skin tingled with awareness. She sensed Wade sorting through all she'd said. Restless, impatient, she put her arms around his neck and pressed her body close to his. He felt so solid, so damn good. But he didn't embrace her. Which made her heart falter. Had she made a mistake? "You see, you were right. There was an unknown factor when I inserted my questionnaire into the computer banks."

He touched her waist. "What was that?"

"I was looking for a soul mate. My very own. I think that's why I really wanted to open Sole Mates in the first place. I think, subconsciously, I realized I was lonely, too. And I didn't want to be alone forever."

"And did you find your soul mate?"

"Oh, yes! Wade Brooks, you are the man for me." Her heart swelled with joy. Then it pinched with fear. He never had answered her question. "Well," she asked, her pulse thundering in her ears, "are you interested in being my groom, my soul mate?"

He stared at her for the longest minute in the *Guinness Book of Records*. Finally, when she thought she would crumble into a million pieces of despair, he captured her mouth with his. His kiss was sudden, deep and all-consuming.

When he pulled away, a cheer went up around them.

"Now, that's what I taught you, Jess." Nina beamed. "To get what you want."

Jack clapped, then hugged Amber close to his side. "Want to make it a double wedding, sis?"

Slowly, the crowd began to disperse, moving away from them and heading toward the refreshments. Wade continued to hold her. Which was a good thing, because if he'd let her go she might have collapsed.

"Jessie, I'm sorry. So sorry, baby. Can you forgive me?"

She gave him a dreamy smile. "If you can go on kissing me like that."

His mouth pulled to the side in a half grin. "My pleasure."

He kissed her until her toes curled and her heart pounded with need. When he looked at her again, his eyes shone like cobalt. "I want you to understand what happened that night we were together."

"I think I know."

"How? I'm not sure I even understand it all myself."

"Because I know you."

"You do?" His hands roamed over her back. "Want to know me better."

She nodded. "When does the honeymoon start?"

"Immediately." His mouth swooped down on hers for a quick kiss.

Then his look turned serious. "You scared the hell out of me, lady."

"I didn't mean to."

"It wasn't you. It was me. I was scared to love you like I loved Tanya. More than I loved Tanya."

Jessie's heart stalled, then opened to new possibilities.

"But I learned over the past weeks that I can't stop from loving you. Because I already do. It's too late. And I realized that Tanya wasn't my true soul mate. She pursued her dreams no matter how it affected me."

"Just like I wanted to race off to secure my bet."

He nodded.

"I'm so sorry, Wade. I didn't think I was taking anything away from us. I thought we were working together."

"I know." He smoothed his hand along her jawline. "It wasn't as if you were leaving for weeks or months, like Tanya. What scared me was how much I needed you." He clasped her hand, entwining their fingers, uniting them. "I realize now that we don't have to sacrifice everything to love each other. We *both* have to compromise. It was lopsided one way in my marriage. And I wanted it lopsided the other way with you. That wasn't fair."

She smiled up at him. "We can have both work and love. I promise I won't be so focused."

"You go right on being focused. That's one of the many things I love about you, Jess."

"But you can't win the bet," Jack intervened.

"Oh, leave them alone," Amber admonished with a playful swat.

"I may have lost the bet, big brother," Jessie said. Raising up on tiptoes, she hooked her arms over Wade's broad shoulders. "But I won the world."

"Does that mean you'll forgive me? And marry me?" Wade asked.

"Yes."

He let out a whoop, then kissed her hard and fast. Releasing her mouth, he gave her a hard stare. "Which question did you answer?"

Grinning, she said, "Both."

Before she could kiss Wade as her groom-to-be, Jack's voice echoed over the P.A. system. "Looks like it's a match, folks. Our first Sole Mate success story." He clapped Wade on the back. "Jessie will have to agree that I predicted it with my theory."

"The shoes worked," Jessie confessed. "Never thought I'd fall for a golfer."

"And I for a career-minded woman." With one arm still wrapped around Jessie's waist, Wade grabbed the microphone. "But Jessie's new computer program made the match, too. Right, Jess?"

Her shoulders tightened for a moment then relaxed. What did it really matter? She once had thought it would be the worst thing in the world to lose a bet and ten percent of her profits to her brother, but not anymore. Not when she was getting the real prize— Wade. She gave a slight shake of her head and said, "No. My program failed."

Jack laughed. "So, fellows," he said into the mike, "step up and register for Sole Mates. My shoe theory will stomp out your bachelor blues."

Wade's brows slanted downward. "But, Jess, you said it matched us up." He gave her waist a squeeze and whispered, "You know, Gertrude and Big Foot."

Turning into her embrace she stared up at the man she loved more than work, more than a bet, more than anything. "Love isn't predictable. My program only matched us when I'd deleted everyone else from the database."

Wade tipped his head back and laughed. Then he looked at her with such tenderness her heart surged. "That means even more to me. Because you defied the odds. You went with your heart."

Her heart led her to kiss him then, knowing she wasn't sacrificing one part of herself but expanding her horizons. For the first time in her life, she felt complete as a woman, whole. All because of Wade.

## Coming in January 2000
### Classics for two of your favorite series.

# SECRET VOWS

by

# REBECCA YORK
&
# KELSEY ROBERTS

From the best of Rebecca York's

**43 Light St.**

## Till Death Us Do Part

Marissa Devereaux discovered that paradise wasn't all it was cracked up to be when she was abducted by extremists on the Caribbean island of Costa Verde.... But things only got worse when Jed Prentiss showed up, claiming to be her fiancé.

From the best of Kelsey Roberts's

**THE ROSE TATTOO**

## Unlawfully Wedded

J.D. was used to getting what he wanted from people, and he swore he'd use that skill to hunt down Tory's father's killer. But J.D. wanted much more than gratitude from his sassy blond bride—and he wasn't going to clue her in. She'd find out soon enough...if she survived to hear about it.

Available January 2000 at your favorite retail outlet.

**HARLEQUIN®**
*Makes any time special* ™

Visit us at www.romance.net

PSBR2200

# *Temptation*®

## COMING NEXT MONTH

### #765 BILLY AND THE KID Kristine Rolofson
**Bachelors & Babies**

Everyone in Cowman's Corner, Montana, believed the baby left on Will "Billy" Wilson's doorstep was his. And Will wasn't saying otherwise. So when Daisy McGregor agreed to help him look after "the kid," she knew she was risking her heart. Because she was looking for a family kind of man—and Will had *no* plans to be a daddy or a husband.

### #766 MILLION DOLLAR VALENTINE Rita Clay Estrada

Mall exec Blake Wright really needed to loosen up. Who better to help out than Crystal Tynan, masseuse and free spirit? Except she seemed to rub him the wrong way...especially when she started getting overly creative with the window dressing of her aunt's flower shop. Still, there *was* a sizzling attraction...and it *was* Valentine's Day.

### #767 VALENTINE FANTASY Jamie Denton

Fantasy For Hire...*Your pleasure is our business!* Newspaper reporter Cait Sullivan was determined to expose this unusual company as a sham, even if it meant going undercover. But once she met sexy-as-sin owner Jordan McBride, all she could think about was getting him "under the covers"....

### #768 BARING IT ALL Sandra Chastain
**Sweet Talkin' Guys**

Reporter Sunny Clary was on a mission—to disclose the true identity of legendary male stripper Lord Sin. Only, every path led her to sexy playboy Ryan Malone. But it was her reaction to the two men that had her confused. Lord Sin made her yearn.... Ryan Malone made her burn.... How could she be drawn to such completely different men? *Or were they so different?*

CNM0100